YOU LET ME IN

www.penguin.co.uk

YOU LET ME IN

Camilla Bruce

BANTAM PRESS

TRANSWORLD PUBLISHERS
61–63 Uxbridge Road, London W5 5SA
www.penguin.co.uk

Transworld is part of the Penguin Random House group of companies
whose addresses can be found at global.penguinrandomhouse.com

Penguin
Random House
UK

First published in Great Britain in 2020 by Bantam Press
an imprint of Transworld Publishers

A CIP catalogue record for this book
is available from the British Library.

ISBNs 9781787633162 hb
9781787633179 tpb

Typeset in 12/15.25pt Adobe Garamond Pro by Jouve (UK), Milton Keynes.
Printed and bound in Great Britain by Clays Ltd, Elcograf S.p.A.

Penguin Random House is committed to a sustainable
future for our business, our readers and our planet. This book
is made from Forest Stewardship Council® certified paper.

YOU LET ME IN

Bestselling Author Disappears Without a Trace

Seventy-four-year-old romance novelist Cassandra Tipp, best known for titles like Golden Suns *and* A Wish for Carrie, *has been missing from her home since at least late August, authorities say. Nothing is known about the prolific author's whereabouts or why she has left her home. The police do not suspect – but cannot rule out – foul play.*

Local deliveryman Brian Frost had no way of knowing that he would be the last person to see the reclusive writer before she disappeared. Cassandra Tipp seemed in good health, even cheery, when she picked up her bags of groceries on the porch of her house in the woods last week.

She had given Mr Frost a handsome tip and a small smile before retiring inside with her oatmeal and tea bags. No one has spoken to her since.

'She definitely didn't look unhappy,' the young man said, commenting on the rumor that the writer chose to end her life in some unknown location.

The S— Police are not so certain. 'Maybe the past came back to haunt her. She has a history here,' Officer William Parks Jr said. The officer is no doubt referring to the trial following her husband's violent death 38 years ago, where Cassandra Tipp was a suspect. The murder and its aftermath launched Mrs Tipp's writing career; her fame partly due to her therapist Dr V. Martin's book about the case, *Away with the Fairies: A Study in Trauma-Induced Psychosis*, which briefly climbed the bestseller lists.

Mrs Tipp's latest novel, *Thorns in November*, was published in June last year to much acclaim and the usual high sales.

A Haunted Life

Cassandra Tipp's family was back in the limelight 27 years ago, when her father and brother tragically died in a supposed murder-suicide. Mrs Tipp was estranged from her family at that point, but the ripples from the tragedy added to her already considerable aura of tristesse. The novel she published that year, *A Wish for Carrie*, became an instant bestseller.

'It is not fair to say that she profited from the tragedy,' book critic and Tipp enthusiast Miranda Hope said, 'but it certainly didn't hurt the numbers either. Everyone wanted a peek inside her head, and her novels gave them just that, even if they were mostly about heated affairs and the promise of true love. Not to say she didn't know how to write,' Hope continued. 'You don't get to publish 42 books if you can't deliver the magic.'

Now Cassandra Tipp herself seems to be the next bead on the string of misfortune that has followed her family for decades – though not everyone is convinced.

'She might not be dead at all,' said Olivia Blatten, sister of the woman in question. 'She always had a flair for drama. She could be anywhere, France or Italy, reading the headlines about herself while sipping a glass of cool wine. It would be just like her. She destroyed our family, you know, ruined it with her shameful lies.'

Mrs Blatten's son, Janus Blatten, was not as harsh in the judgment of his aunt. 'She is not so young anymore. Maybe she just wanted to retire with a bang.'

The S— Police do not endorse this theory. 'She has not been in contact with anyone since the last week of August,' Officer Parks said. 'There has not been any activity in her bank accounts or calls made from her phone. We do not know when and we do not know how, but we are convinced that Cassandra Tipp is dead.'

INSTRUCTIONS REGARDING THE LAST WILL AND TESTAMENT OF CASSANDRA TIPP

1. Only Cassandra Tipp's named heirs, Janus and Penelope Blatten, son and daughter of her estranged sister, Olivia Blatten, can claim the estate.

2. In the event of Cassandra Tipp's natural or accidental death, her estate can be claimed immediately.

3. Should Cassandra Tipp go missing, a year must pass from the day she was last seen or heard from before a claim can be made.

4. When or if that happens, Cassandra Tipp's heirs must complete the following steps to secure the transaction of the estate:
   — Go to Cassandra Tipp's residence.
   — Enter the study on the ground floor.
   — Read the manuscript left for them on the desk.
   — Within the manuscript is a password that must be verbally communicated to the estate's executive, Mr Owen Norris, with Norris, Norris and Nesbit, in order for the claim to be valid.

5. One or both parties can claim the estate.

6. Should one of the parties choose not to claim the estate, this must be conveyed in writing, signed by the party and two witnesses. The party's share of the estate will pass on to their sibling.

7. If none of the parties claims the estate, Mr Norris will sell all assets and ensure that all funds belonging to the estate will benefit various organizations (list enclosed).

Signed,

Cassandra Tipp

Written by

CASSANDRA TIPP

1

You drive up the dirt road between the old oak trees. It's October, so I guess it must be raining. Maybe there's a wind blowing too, leaving yellow leaves on your windshield. You scan your surroundings keenly on the way, check the mirrors for signs of life, but find none. There are no neighbors here, no Sunday strollers. It's only you two and the dirt road, the leafy forest around you, ancient trees with wide trunks and gnarled bark, coiling roots and branches.

The road ends right at my porch, so that is where you're coming to a halt. You park the car by the empty hen-house and give my humble home a long, hard stare. Janus, you step out of the car first, maybe you take off your sunglasses or tussle your thinning hair. Penelope, you purse your lips and shield your eyes from the sun with your hand, even though it's cloudy. Your high heel sinks into the soggy ground, catches yellow strands of wizened grass and, maybe, an old and tattered hen feather.

Neither of you says anything I think, not at first. You just stand there for a while, looking up at the three-story building; the multitude of windows, some square, some round, the flaking paint in a light shade of lilac. She's a magical house, but she isn't pretty. She's like an overdone birthday cake gone stale, old frosting sliding off the edges. The apple and cherry trees that flank her on both sides have long since ceased blooming and touch the walls with black, spindly fingers. This time of year they serve mostly as the home of spiders. In the windows, you see sheets of old lace and heavy drapes of bottle-green velvet.

Janus, you shake your head, give your sister a telling look, and mumble under your breath: 'Crazy Aunt Cassie. I never knew it was this bad . . .'

You step gingerly onto the porch then, unsure if the old boards will hold your weight. Janus, you take the key from your pocket. My solicitor gave it to you this very morning with a sheet of instructions. Maybe he laughed a little when he gave it to you, apologized even, saying something along the lines of 'The old lady went a little soft before she vanished.' He doesn't like me much, Mr Norris. The feeling is in every way mutual.

You are good kids, however, so it would never occur to you not to follow the instructions that I left you, and that is why you are at the house, carefully crossing the deck of my porch. The lock on the front door gives in to the key with a clicking sound, and the door itself swings open on creaking hinges. Penelope wrinkles up her nose at the scent of old and musty, thinly veiled with lavender and thyme, that greets you when you step inside.

In the hallway, you look upon rows of hats and coats and shawls, hanging from hooks on the walls. They are horribly outdated – old woman's clothes. Penelope smiles when she gazes upon straw hats with flowers and wax fruits attached to the pull. Her soft fingers with the dark red nails swiftly touch the handle of my black umbrella, the yellowing lace of a shawl. Even when young I had vintage tastes.

Janus doesn't dally. He swiftly strides further inside, takes it all in: the black painted stairs to the next floor, the dusty chandelier with three dozen prisms, the open kitchen door that gives you a glimpse of the black-and-white-checked floor. Penelope's nose wrinkles up again when she imagines cupboards filled with stale food, but not to worry, Penelope, I have taken care of all that.

At this point, I think, your tongues are less tied:

'Sure could do with a dusting,' one of you, I'm guessing Janus, says when you enter the parlor, his hand resting lightly on my champagne-colored sofa. Penelope walks straight to the bookcase that runs from floor to ceiling, her red nails trailing old spines. She is a librarian, after all, and books are like honey and cream to her. Down on the floor, her high heels leave marks on the dusty floorboards.

'Where is her study, then?' Janus looks around the room, the sheet of instructions crumpled between his fingers. It says to go to the study, but you, poor hatchlings, don't know where that study is, so you are left there, standing, looking around the room. Hoping for some sign or clue to point you in the right direction.

'These are her books,' Penelope says, having found the row of pink-backed novels on their special shelf.

'How could a childless widow write so much about romance and love?' Janus comes up behind her – maybe.

Penelope shrugs. 'Fiction is sometimes better than reality, don't you think?'

'Perhaps.' Now *he* shrugs. 'I still think it's strange, though.'

'I think it's even stranger that she wrote about such romantic things, considering—'

'Considering what?'

'What she was accused of. If we believe it to be true.'

'That was a very long time ago.' Janus doesn't want to think about all that. Such things are messy and uncomfortable and he is a very neat boy.

'Come on, then,' says Penelope, 'let's find this mysterious study.' She will be craving a cigarette at this point, be eager to get things over with so she can attend to her vices. She knows better, of course, being a modern woman in an aging body, but not even the dreaded forty can make her quit her beloved cigarettes, wrinkled skin or not.

Back in the hall, there is only one door left to try, and lo and behold, it's the study in there; my large oaken desk – not so polished anymore, typewriters hidden beneath thick plastic covers, a chunky old laptop, and windows framed by velvet drapes. Behind the desk is a wide wicker chair, heaped with hard pillows in green silk, matching the hand-painted wallpaper where vines dance like charmed snakes, sprouting fat and glossy leaves. Penelope is instantly taken, trails the vines with her fingertips.

Janus's gaze travels further, and takes in the pieces of wood, roots, and pebbles littering the windowsills; the taxidermy viper mounted on the wall, scales like hard nails, black eyes peering. He sees all the glass jars filled with dried flowers, sometimes a dead moth, sometimes a rock, lined up neatly on the shelf behind the desk, and then, at last, he sees *this*: a stack of pink paper, typed out by yours truly, lying there like a marzipan cake, all ready to be sliced and eaten. Neither of you looks at the room after that. Your eyes are glued to this pink shape.

'There it is,' one of you says.

'That must be it,' says the other.

Janus's hand reaches for it first, Penelope's red nails follow quickly. Both of you read your names on the top sheet. Penelope lifts it away.

And now, here you are. You're standing in my study, holding this story in your hands – the last one I'll ever tell. That means I've been gone for more than a year and that my whereabouts are still unknown, as that was my agreement with Mr Norris. Within these pages is the key to unlock my last will and testament, the secret word that will make Mr Norris open that thick manila envelope and tell you how rich you've become. If you can't find it, there'll be no prize and my money will go elsewhere.

It's a drag, I know. But sometimes the world is just cruel. And you do want to know, don't you? Want to know if those stories your mother told you are true. If I really killed them all. If I am that mad.

This is the story as I recall it, and yours now too, to guard or treasure or forget as you please. I wanted someone to know, you see. To know my truth, now that I am gone.

How everything and none of it happened.

2

I have sometimes been asked why I remained in S— after the trial. After the man you knew as Tommy Tipp died. It would have been so easy then, to slip away and move somewhere else, to a town or a city where people didn't know me. A *clean slate* was what Dr Martin prescribed.

A fresh start.

Of course, I didn't particularly *like* staying in S—. All the eyes staring when I walked down the street or bought ground beef and carrots at the grocery store. My name had been on everyone's lips for months, my face gracing the front pages. If they didn't know me before, they certainly did by then. But I had reasons, as you'll come to understand.

And things weren't quite as they seemed.

Tommy Tipp was not what you think he was.

I know you liked him, he was always good to you children. I remember him taking Janus fishing and spinning with Penelope on the lawn. You picked him flowers once, do you remember, Penelope, those daisies and bluebells you gave him? Even your mother warmed to him, eventually. Told me how happy she was that I had finally found 'an ounce of happiness', that I was 'settling down' – even with Tommy Tipp.

They were mystified, I think, Olivia and her friends, and Mother too, as to why Tommy Tipp chose me. He was dashingly handsome in a dangerous way with a shock of blond hair and very blue eyes, body lean and skin tanned. He was the man all the women in S— dreamed of at night while lying in their husbands' arms. He was at the center of that guilty, sweet lust they could not curb, no matter how respectable, how well adjusted and successful they were. Tommy Tipp could ignite a fire in virgins and widows alike. Married women were his specialty; they cost him very little both in effort and in risk. Before he met me, he made a business of it, sleeping around for gifts and favors. He was a champion of secret daytime trysts, every one of the women thinking herself the only one. We all knew he had been to prison, of course, that his past was littered with battery and theft. S— is a small town. But who doesn't love a redeemed villain, an angel with the alluring taint of sin? I never was so blind, never wanted him for being dangerous; I already had a dangerous lover – already knew the taste of sin. No wonder the ladies were cross, though, when his gorgeous body was found in the woods.

But I'm moving too fast, we're not there yet. A lot of things happened before that.

***

One thing you must know: I was never a *good* girl.

Never like your mother, all compliant and soft. She reveled in praise, that one, twinkled like a star when someone told her she did well. I was the awkward older sister, ungainly and thin where she was soft and round. Olivia's hair shone like polished copper, mine was wavy and brown. Her skin was like milk, mine marred by freckles, but a sprinkle of pigments makes no bad girl, of course, it runs deeper than that, runs in the blood. Some of us are just born *wrong*.

Your mother would have told you we were never close.

How we were never the same, she and I. Especially after the rumors and, of course, after the trial, she was eager to forsake me.

I remember it differently, though. I remember summer vacations spent at the seaside, small golden anchors pinned to our chests. I remember looking through the glass-like water in shallow ponds, teasing crabs, collecting seashells. I remember sand between our toes, sweet ice cream melting on our tongues. I remember cake on the porch, fat pieces of fruit embedded like jewels in the sponge. The setting sun before us bleeding a golden light that turned her hair into a coppery river, turned her milky skin a darker, softer shade.

I remember the dolls we got one Christmas morning; pale skinned and black of hair. The home we made for them under the dining room table; white walls of tablecloth, eggcups as goblets and silken pillows as thrones. Medieval princesses both. We picked roses in the garden and adorned their hair, wrought thorny stems as crowns, and had our brother, Ferdinand, serenade them with his recorder, which he played with zeal if not delight.

I remember laughing together, like sisters.

I remember that, and more.

Olivia would tell you it never happened.

Maybe she's forgotten that it did.

3

Mother was a stern woman, maybe not too happy. Her hair when she was young was a mass of yellow curls, her lips painted a stark shade of red. Her body was lithe and very thin. She liked to wear pencil skirts in dark blue and bright red. Her boat-neck sweaters were striped or dotted. Her everyday jewels were pieces of glass set in cheap frames; pure colors and pearls of polished metal. Her shoes had high but sensible heels; thick stubs, not thin spikes. Her nylons never tore.

Father was a big man with fleshy lips and cheeks like a basset hound. His skin held a shade between scarlet and blue. Stars like fireworks bloomed on his cheeks where vessels had erupted. He used to be a boxer back in the day, but after *we* arrived, his litter of cubs, he was a salesman honing a taste for vodka.

I sometimes imagine the two of them meeting by the ring, floor stained with sweat and spit, a spatter of crimson blood. His body was fit then; hard muscles and slick skin. She was perky and young, nothing but lips and tits. Sometimes I think I was already there when they met, hidden in the hot, dark cave of my mother's belly. As a child, I dearly wished it to be so. As an adult, it's just speculation. What is true, though, is that I arrived into this world a little too soon after the wedding bells rang.

Mother brought some money with her into the marriage. She always had class, if not the brains to play it smart. Hers was the remains of old money, shipping money, steeped in the sweat and labor of others. As the only child of an only child the money was hers by right. It made her feel entitled, I think. Made her feel there was something to lose. She carried with her a picture of who she thought she ought to be – who we *all* ought to be. Falling in love with a boxer had clearly not been a part of her plan. She'd had a 'phase', I think now, back when they met, raging against the confinements of society.

He was different, a simple man, fueled by quiet anger. I'm sure it was no coincidence that he ended up in that ring. If he hadn't met my mother, he probably would've been happy enough just working at the docks. Instead my father sold things: machinery mostly, expensive farm equipment, lawnmowers. We always kept a lovely garden. Our house was very white. We had help because Mother's back was broken from carrying us children. Our surroundings were always spotless; fresh flowers in every vase, white surfaces unmarred by clutter. I think she needed that to keep calm, to feel an ounce of control. She always seemed to me a string wound too tight. One day it would snap, and we would all be in trouble.

My younger brother Ferdinand was a quiet boy, chewing his emotions. Honey hair and blushing cheeks. He was good at chess, but neither of my parents saw any value in that. He took up fencing for a while, but I think the weapons scared him. It always unnerved me, the silence in that boy, or maybe I'm only saying that now because I know what happened later.

And then there was Olivia; round of cheek, sweet as marzipan, protected by her own radiance. She was the image my mother had in mind when she set about producing children. It took her three tries to get one like that. When she saw what became of your mother, though, I imagine she probably cried. She could never have envisioned her golden child to grow so dull, didn't pay for those ballet lessons and acting classes so Olivia would go on to be a mere housewife. She was supposed to accomplish, I think. Do those things our mother could not because she went and had us. Olivia was supposed to make a name for herself, be a movie star or a woman of the world. Have expensive lunches, host fundraisers for orphans, and click her way across marble floors in very expensive shoes.

Olivia blames me for how things turned out. How could she ever be all that, with my notoriety hanging around her neck?

I have ruined it all for her, haven't I? Forced her to dwell in the shadows.

Forced you all to dwell in the shadows.

I am not sorry for that.

It's not like I had any choice, you know, and even if I did, I might not have acted any differently. There was always a distance between them and me. They didn't see what I saw, didn't know what I knew. And maybe there's some resentment in there too, because what my mother failed so spectacularly to see was how vulnerable it all made me. How I was like a raw egg, all tender and fragile, so easy to break.

No one keeps an eye on the bad girl. The peculiar daughter is left on her own. So easy to slip away then, fall into the twilight places of the world. To be taken and lost. Preyed upon.

Good girls smell like burnt tangerines for those with bad intentions – fragrant but bitter, it is a repellant. Bad girls like me smell like ripe apples, ready for picking, juicy and tart.

No one will miss them at all.

But I could have used a mother's protection.

4

This I remember: the horrid sound when the flowerpot crashed to the floor. I was five at the time, standing by the living room window, bright sunlight was streaming inside, and thin white curtains billowed in the breeze. My companion – my only friend – smiled at me, a toothy grin.

I called him 'Pepper-Man', for the strong scent that emitted from him, warning me of his arrival. Usually he would appear at the end of my bed, sat there cross-legged, grooming his hair with a comb made from bone, or twisting twigs into animals and crowns; gifts for his little girl.

His skin was gray and gnarled, black warts clustered at his joints, his long white hair hung nearly to his knees, ragged and dry as old hay. He was very tall. His fingers were long. They had just swept the newly filled flowerpot off the white-painted windowsill and now his dark eyes, the color of moss, were watching the door expectantly – curious.

Pepper-Man's black lips drew back from his teeth when my mother came into the room. The gray tatters that clothed his ungainly body shifted and moved in the draft from the door.

'Oh, Cassie,' my mother said, hands on the hips of her navy-blue skirt. 'Why do you keep doing that? I told you to leave those flowers *alone*.' Her gaze was on the red petunia, petals crushed by dirt and pottery shards.

'It wasn't me.' I twisted my sweaty hands in the skirt of my yellow summer dress. 'It was Pepper-Man—'

'Oh, won't you stop with that already.' She crossed the floor swiftly, mid-sized heels clicking on the floorboards. 'Where is this *Pepper-Man*, then? Flew out the window?' She bent down, collecting sharp pieces of pottery in her hand. My friend was towering above her, still with that curiosity in his gaze, that smile plastered to his black lips.

'No,' I said, breathless, watched as my mother's stiff hair nearly brushed Pepper-Man's body when she straightened up again.

'You are a big girl now, Cassie,' said Mother. 'I think it's time you stopped blaming someone else for your mistakes. This is the fifth flowerpot this week, why can't you just leave them be? What did the poor flowers ever do to you?'

'Nothing,' I muttered, my gaze on the floor, where Mother's black and shiny shoes stood next to the twisted toes of my friend. I just wanted her to go away, didn't trust Pepper-Man around other people. He was capricious and sometimes cruel, too curious about everything. His hand reached now, for the top of her head; fingers flexing, rubbing together; long nails stretching through the air. 'They are stupid,' I said quickly, to grab her attention and get her away from Pepper-Man's fingers. 'I hate the flowers! They are stupid flowers! They are ugly and red and I hate them!' I spun around, grabbed another flowerpot from the windowsill, this one topped with fluffy, white blossoms, and threw it hard to the floor. Dirt spattered everywhere. This pot didn't break but rolled across the floor, coming to a halt by my mother's feet. Pepper-Man's hand retracted.

'Cassie!' Mother cried, dropping the broken shards she

held. They landed on the floor, in the heap of dirt and greenery. 'Look what you made me do.' She held up a finger. Fat droplets of blood trailed her white skin, aiming for her golden rings.

'Good,' I said and stomped my foot. Pepper-Man's thin nostrils flared, his black tongue came out to lick his lips. He liked blood a lot. It made him perk up like a dog with a treat. It felt like a stab to my tiny chest watching him watch her like that, so I ran. I brushed past her, tears streaming, and slammed the door behind me; up the stairs; feet like drumsticks, into my room, where I threw myself on top of the bed and let my tears soak into the mattress.

Pepper-Man was already there, as I knew he'd be. That was the point of the whole charade, to lure him away from Mother. He sat perched on top of my crocheted bedspread, humming a gentle tune; fingers braiding, twisting, and shaping the birch twigs in his hands. He didn't look at me, didn't have to.

Ours was an intimate relationship.

***

I cannot recall a world without Pepper-Man; he has always been around me, coming and going, mostly just there. Sometimes a menace, other times bliss. Pepper-Man is very old.

Once, he told me he had found me as a toddler, playing on the banks by the river. He had been floating downstream, he said, when he caught sight of my gleaming hair in the meadow. My mother and father, young then and still in love, were having a picnic nearby. He said they had sandwiches and pears, drank tea from painted china. He was riding the water on an oak leaf when he saw me sitting there alone, all round cheeked and plump. He wanted me, he said, so he jumped.

When I said I didn't believe that he would want me like that, for no reason at all, he laughed and said that all of his kind wanted hair like mine to stroke and braid and play with, but maybe I was right.

In truth, he said, he had been traveling the sky as a crow at the time, his bird's eyes trailing the ground for prey. He was very hungry, he said, for meat. Then he saw me, just a baby then, lying alone outside our home. He swept down and perched on the edge of my basket, talons curling around the edge. He thought I had the loveliest eyes, and wondered how they'd taste. But then my mother came out and shooed at him, chasing him away. He said that was why he remained with me; still wondered about the taste of my eyes, how it would feel to have them slip down his throat.

I didn't quite believe that, either, and told him as much. Why would he wait so long to eat them, if my eyes made his stomach growl like that? He laughed again, said I might be right, and told me I'd tripped on a faerie mound. He'd been strolling nearby, minding his own business, when a terrible wail rose from the ground. That was me, knees bruised and hands dirty, white dress all ruined. He felt sorry for me then, and wanted to make me something pretty, like a wreath of flowers or a crown of twigs, but then my mother and father came rushing and carried me away, shushing and kissing and tending my wounds. He followed me home and slipped inside, making me gifts ever since.

There is another story too, where Pepper-Man and I are born from the same pod. Siblings in spirit if not in flesh, forever connected through unbreakable bonds. We are the same, he and I, even if we don't share DNA. We have always been together and will always remain so.

I will not speak of that other option, so brazenly launched at the murder trial. There will be time for that later. Unlike the others, the latter was not among the stories I heard as a child, when I was lying in his hard arms, breathing against his still chest, his dry hair a blanket, his pepper scent a comfort, feeling the paper-thin leather of his pointed ears against my fingertips as I trailed their shape against the lace of my pillows. His voice sounded only in my head; a soft whisper, like wind rustling in leaves. I used to close my eyes and drift on the sound of his voice, losing myself in its rise and fall. Like being submerged under water, that feeling; that falling into him. A rattle would start at the base of my spine and push its way through my body; push and push, rattle and shake, until I split open and rushed from my skin; sped like a lightning bolt through the roof, toward the sky, while images and noises flashed past me. I saw people I hadn't seen before walking unfamiliar streets. Once, it was a woman in a black coat looking through her purse, the pavement under her feet was cobbled, the buildings surrounding her made of brick. Another time it was a man with a mustard-colored tie, chasing a blue bus. The bus driver glanced at him in the mirror and drove on, while the man stomped his foot and threw his hat to the ground. I saw children with brown skin in a playground, wearing gray uniforms, munching soft candy. And other things too, twisting, coiling among the roots of ancient trees: pale snakes and old women licking black juice from the trunks, men with goat's heads running through the woods, and girls with snapping jaws spinning dresses from spider silk in hot, dry caves underground. Sometimes I was at sea, moving with the waves, salt on my lips and seaweed in my hair, moving with the shadows beneath me.

When I woke up from these trips, Pepper-Man was always there, his teeth buried deep in my throat. He lifted his head to whisper in my ear: 'I love you, Cassie, I do. You taste like the finest buttercups and wine.'

***

At Sunday dinner it was Mother who poured the wine, letting it slouch off the rim and down on the table. Her lips were crusted with crimson. There were chicken and mashed potatoes. Caramel pudding for dessert. In this memory, I am eight years old.

'Eat,' she wheezed at me. Her eyes were shiny and blue. They reminded me of the stained-glass window at church. The one with Mary and the baby, the color being the only likeness. The pearls around her neck swung back and forth between her breasts; cool white globes, shimmering and hard.

Father asked: 'What has Cassandra done now?'

Mother lifted her hands in exasperation. 'Well, look at her! Look at that hair. Why couldn't she at least *try* to comb it before church?' In truth, I had given up on that hair. Pepper-Man kept twisting it at night, braiding it and curling it, licking it even, with his long, black tongue.

'What does it matter?' Father's eyes were bloodshot, his tie all askew.

'People will think I run *a zoo*,' said Mother. 'They'll think I have no control over my children.' Her hand shook as she fetched the salt.

'There is nothing wrong with Cassandra's hair,' said Father.

'Nothing wrong? It's a wilderness. And it's not just the hair. Her clothes are stained and her knees are bruised. Why can't you ever be neat, Cassie? Why do you always have to ruin everything?'

'Cassie is bad,' said Olivia, only five then. Her feet under the table shot out and hit those bruised knees.

'That's right, Olivia.' Mother's voice went sweet but not warm; she stretched a linen napkin between her fingers, pulled until the fabric strained. 'Promise me you'll never be like your sister.'

'I'll never be like my sister,' said Olivia. *Her* neat braids were tipped with velvet bows.

'Maybe she's waiting for *a bird* to come flying and nest up there.' Mother's voice verged on hysteria; she was looking at my hair again. Suddenly she laughed, or cried, it was hard to know the difference.

'Maybe not so much wine,' tried Father.

'Maybe I wouldn't *need* all this wine if she could only behave!' She didn't look at me at all.

Ferdinand, seven at the time, pushed his food around on his plate. 'I don't feel well,' he said. 'May I be excused?'

'No,' Mother snapped, 'you may not be excused. You may stay put and eat your pudding.'

Something dark entered Father's gaze. 'Go on,' he said to Ferdinand. 'You may be excused.'

'What?' cried Mother. 'He did that very same thing *last* Sunday—'

'And you drank too much wine then, too, and picked on Cassandra, just like you're doing now.'

'Well.' Mother rose from her chair, the napkin fluttered to the floor. '*Someone* has to discipline her.'

Father started to laugh then. It was a deep and scary sound, like those first rolls of thunder on a warm summer's day.

5

So, what is this to you, you may ask? This isn't the story you expected. You were expecting a repenting sinner's last confession. Expecting me to cry on the page, admit my wrongdoings and beg your forgiveness. Instead you get this: childhood memories. I am sorry about that – sorry to disappoint, but the truth of it is, I cannot recall a world without Pepper-Man in it, and him being in it was the beginning of it all.

We will get to the bodies eventually.

***

I remember elementary school as a string of days of aching belly and sleep deprivation, a fear that my classmates or teachers would somehow see through me and figure out how I spent my nights. See it and punish me, like Mother did. You'd think it would make me shy, wouldn't you? Think it would make me seek out the shadows, but it didn't. It made me angry.

It wasn't easy to blend in with a companion like Pepper-Man. The other girls in S— were sensible creatures stuffed in ruffles and lace. They had well-groomed hair and polished manners. Much like Olivia: *good* to the core. Mother was most adamant I kept quiet about it all: my visits in the woods, the sharp nibs at my flesh, and the gifts of bones and feathers that I got. I was never to speak of, draw, or in any other way express my wraith's existence.

'They'll think you're mad,' she told me. 'They'll think you're mad and then they'll lock you up.' I didn't want that, of course, so I tried the best I could to abide by her rules. But it wasn't easy. I was straddling two worlds: the one everyone could see, and the one that was forbidden. No child should be subjected to a fate like that. It wears you so thin, is such a burden. There is shame in there too, in that sense of being *wrong*.

And I was always worried that Pepper-Man would hurt someone. He was a wild thing on a leash, my friend, something I ought to, but could not, control.

It was quite a mission for a very young girl. A dreadful responsibility.

I remember Mother's pale face when yet another parent had been at our door with her crying daughter in tow. I'd seen Pepper-Man watching her one day when he walked me to school. This girl, Carol, had been out playing in the schoolyard with the sunlight illuminating her butter-colored curls. Pepper-Man paused by the wrought-iron fence and looked at her for a very long time. The hunger I saw in his gaze then worried me so much I decided I'd rather just hurt her first, before he had time to braid her a crown and sink his teeth into her neck.

I was nine then, one of my worst years. Pepper-Man had been a snarling beast all winter, dancing around me always. I fell asleep with his teeth in my throat more often than not. He took to ogling Olivia's fresh-faced friends with hunger in his gaze, even Olivia herself, with her polished copper braids. No matter how often he tasted me, it never seemed to quench his thirst. No matter what I did to appease him – telling him how I loved him, how much his gifts meant to me – he never seemed to be satisfied. I think I screamed and thrashed and lashed at those girls just so Pepper-Man wouldn't. He had promised he needed only me, after all. Had promised me I was his only princess. The red marks that I left on their skin were warning signs, what little pain my scratching nails, hard little fists, and teeth could inflict were really nothing in comparison to what *he* could do.

'How dare you?' Mother cried at me, all flushed and angry, reading another letter from my deeply concerned teacher. 'How dare you ruin our reputation like that? Fighting like a street rat! They'll think you have no manners – no manners at all!'

I was rinsing beans by the kitchen table, guided by our housekeeper Fabia's stern hand. Pepper-Man was sitting on the kitchen counter, *sprawling*, more like it, long limbs extended on the clean surface; he looked like a spider, gray and spindly. I didn't give a word in reply. What was there to say?

Mother shook her head, didn't look as angry anymore, more afraid, or sad. 'This won't end well, Cassie. Not for you, not for anyone. Just think of your brother, what this will do to him. He doesn't react well to all this upheaval.'

I nodded once. We both already knew there was disaster in the brewing.

'You are jealous, I think,' Pepper-Man said that same night, as he folded me in his embrace. 'You do not want me to taste another, you want me to have only you.'

I reddened then, beneath the covers. I didn't want it to be true. 'You'll hurt them,' I said. 'You'll make them bleed.'

'But so, my love, do you.'

Just as I said, two peas in a pod. We were always the same, my Pepper-Man and I.

***

I should have been unhappy that the other girls didn't like me, but I wasn't. I had many other friends to occupy my time, way more entertaining than my classmates. I was seven, maybe eight, the first time Pepper-Man took me to see his kin. It was early autumn, the leaves on the trees barely tinged with yellow. It was a Saturday, I believe, since I was home from school but had not been to church and the household was preparing for a dinner that night. Mother, always the perfectionist, was on a mission to make our home as spotless as possible before the important event. In consequence, she and Fabia were tearing my room apart. They had removed all the books from my shelves, laid them out in colorful rows on the soft white carpet on the floor. Golden-haired, red-lipped heroines and dark-haired side-kicks were grinning up at me from the covers. Mother and Fabia were looking for what was hidden behind them.

'Why do you keep doing this?' my mother complained, tossing wreaths of birch and oak, jewelry of bone and fur, down on the floor by my feet. Fabia held half a robin's eggshell between two fingers, pinching her nose lightly. I looked down. There was a bracelet of dead raspberry leaves, a ring made from deer spine, a necklace of frogs' legs and hawthorn. It was the debris from these gifts that gave them away. My mother couldn't stand clutter, and natural matter tends to leave a trail, especially in a very white room.

I kept silent, bit my lower lip. I knew it would do no good at all, telling them the truth. The older I got, the less patient my mother grew with Pepper-Man and his antics. Telling her that these were his gifts would only anger her more.

'We can buy some nice glass beads,' she said. 'If you really want to make things, there are classes for that. You could learn embroidery, or knitting.'

Fabia bent down and looked in under the bed, her scrawny behind jutting out in the room, auburn hair bun bobbing. 'Oh,' she uttered, pulling forth a gaggle of fresh finds: owls' eyes, dried up and shriveled in a nest of roughly woven twigs. A crown made from pine needles and apple wood, a bird made from rowan and daisies.

'If you want to keep running around in the woods alone, you have to stop bringing these things home,' said Mother. 'What do you want all these dead things for, anyway? It's not pretty, Cassie. It's repulsive.'

I didn't disagree.

Fabia crossed herself as she tossed a pendant of claws and teeth onto the growing heap. Mother caught her in the act.

'Don't be foolish,' she said curtly. 'They were already dead when Cassie found them, weren't they, Cassie?' I nodded. 'She isn't *that* mad,' Mother muttered, sending me a furious look.

They tore apart the bed next; fluffy pillows in lace casings, sheets and mattress, everything was thrown to the floor.

'Oh, Cassie, *again?*' Mother complained when she saw the rusty stains I so stealthily had tried to hide, first by scrubbing the mattress with a washcloth, then by turning it over. 'I don't get where this comes from, why won't you tell me?' She was looking me over, searching my skin for scabs. I rubbed my neck, knowing very well that like Pepper-Man himself, she couldn't see the damage done. I could, though. Every day in the mirror, I could see the traces of his love, etched onto my skin in deep punctures. The wounds were just as much part of me as the color of my hair, or the freckles on my nose – just there, and there was nothing I could do about it.

Fabia caught my mother's eyes, motioned discreetly to her lower region.

'No, no, no,' Mother shook her head, 'it's far too early for that.'

Fabia gave me a lingering look and pulled a pair of yellow rubber gloves from the pocket of her apron, started filling the trash bag with gifts.

Mother stood before me, towering above me. 'Is that all?' she asked in her sternest voice. 'Talk to me,' she implored when I just stood there, wringing my hands in my skirt. 'Why won't you say something, Cassie?'

I shook my head, looked down at my toes.

'No excuses? No apologies?'

I kept shaking my head. Why should I have to apologize for what Pepper-Man did? I even felt a bit sorry for him, all his lovely gifts tossed and burned.

'Maybe your teacher is right,' Mother said in a quiet voice when Fabia left with the bag. 'Maybe you ought to see a doctor – the *special* kind.' She made it sound like a threat. 'I don't know what to do with you.' Her hands were on her hips now, fingernails like claws on the slick navy fabric. 'I give you everything a girl could want, a lovely room with lovely toys, a wardrobe filled with dresses, and what do I get in return? Dead frogs and brown leaves, a goddamn forest under your mattress—'

'I don't want your stupid toys,' I told her, lifted my gaze and met hers. Suddenly I was furious, outraged at the unfairness of me being punished like that, all my things scattered and tossed, when *he* was the one who did it. *He* was the one who brought the gifts inside. *He* was the one who said to hide it.

'Well, I can see that,' said Mother. Even in her rage, her curls stayed all in place. 'You would rather have eyes for marbles and rowan sticks for dolls.'

'They are pretty,' I muttered, eyes on the floor again.

'They are dirty and crude, and sometimes they rot.' She was referring to an incident that same spring, when a discarded crow's corpse went bad behind a set of classic fairytales. 'Why won't you just stop?' she sighed and sat down on my stripped bed. For a moment I almost felt sorry for my mother then, she looked so tired and vulnerable, eyes so honest and blue. But pity was a feeling I just couldn't afford.

'Why won't you leave me alone?' I raged, pulled the white ribbon from my hair and threw it at her. It landed like a silken snake across her navy thighs. She picked it up and let it slide between her fingers, a thoughtful expression on her face.

'I put that in so you would look nice tonight,' she told me. 'Father's business associates are coming, you know that. I want us all to look our best.'

'Why?'

'Because it's important that Father makes a good impression.' She reached the ribbon back to me. 'Put it in . . . Go on . . .'

'I'd rather wear a turd on my head,' I said and stomped my foot, to no dramatic effect on the white carpet.

'I know you would.' Voice weary. 'But just for tonight, Cassie, please be your best—'

'Maybe you should just hide me away up here,' I said. 'Maybe you should leave me alone!'

'Yes,' she said, rising from the bed, lips a thin red line. 'Maybe you're right, maybe you should stay here for a while and think about what you've done.' She crossed the floor, paused in the doorway. 'Put everything back in order,' she said, looking at the torn-up room. 'You will be spending quite some time up here.' She went outside and closed the door. I could hear her footsteps as she disappeared down the hall, and later when she came back, jingling with the set of keys, heard her turn one in my door. Locking away the embarrassment that was me. I am sure she let out a breath of relief.

Unbidden tears formed in my eyes then, and I was sobbing as I hauled the mattress back onto the bedframe, dripping salt down on the bloodstains. I could hear the preparations downstairs: furniture pushed across the floor, bottles clinking together while they were put out on display. My father's dark voice was a murmur through the floorboards, and young Olivia's cheery voice giggled at something he said.

I shuddered.

I sat down on my unmade bed, pulled up my knees and cried, looked around at the mess Mother's search had left. The books on the floor and the contents of emptied drawers: coloring pencils, notebooks, a collection of seashells and marbles littered the white sea of my floor.

I fell asleep on the bed, hugging my pillow.

I woke up due to the smell.

The room had grown dark around me; night had arrived. A cold draft came in through the window. Downstairs, I could hear them all, laughing and talking. Glasses clinked together; cutlery met china. But it was the peppery scent that engulfed me, and kept my attention enthralled.

My friend was with me, sitting by my side.

When Pepper-Man saw I was awake, he lifted a hand and put it on top of my head, tousling my hair in silent sympathy.

'They tore everything up,' I told him. 'They threw all your gifts away.'

'Not to worry,' he said in my head. 'I can make new gifts.'

'She will only find and throw away those, too,' I said.

'Then I will make even more.' His black lips split in a grin; his murky eyes blinked. A wreath of blackthorn twigs rested on his white, white hair. He took it off then, and placed it on my head instead. 'You are my princess. It does not matter what your mother says or does, you will always, always have me.'

I smiled and touched the wreath he'd just given me, felt the prickly thorns against my skin. 'They're having a party down-stairs,' I said. 'But *she* has locked me up – I can't go.'

'Would you like to?' His fingers were on my knee, caress-ing it softly.

'No, it's a stupid thing. But I would like to eat. And I really need to pee.'

'Come with me, then, we will have a feast of our own, down by birch and brook, deep in the stones.'

'But I am locked up.'

'We won't go through that door.'

'How will we go, then?' I looked at him wide-eyed.

He nodded to the window.

'It's too far down. I can't jump, I'll break a leg.'

'Ride on my back, then,' he told me – and I did. I clung to his scrawny backside as his spindly legs entered the win-dowsill and the cold night air hit my skin. Pepper-Man crouched there, with me on his back, then he swung us both into the night.

***

A word on faeries, because I think you might be confused: they are not what you think they are. It always baffles me to see faeries in films and recent novels. Either they are happy elementals, strolling about in the woods looking after all living creatures like guardians of the earth, or they're an alien race living among us since time immemorial, hiding behind some veil or deep underground; monsters, pagan gods, and stuff of nightmares. The latter is the more correct approach, of course. People used to be afraid of them; they stole milk and children, abducted brides and handsome men, tricked and cursed. Nothing to love. Fairytales were warnings, not an invitation.

Faeries are neither alien nor truly inhuman, though. They are just no longer alive.

Not that all dead people are faeries. I have come to believe that it's all about the will to life, the strength of the Ki, the power of one's essence. They are not the walking dead of movies, either, but spirits that have transformed and morphed into something new, a different kind of being. Faeries rarely remember ever being human; some barely look like people anymore. They live in the wild and feed off the land, attach themselves to life like leeches. They adopt traits and manners from their sources of life: trees, brooks, animals, us. They are a ragged band; some ugly, some strange. None of them are shimmering, unless they live near water, few of them have gossamer wings, unless they feed off dragonflies. I have never experienced them as particularly wise or kind. How clever can a farmer from the seventh century be, even after some hundred years living as a fox-hugging faerie? Still, they retain some humanity, a *root*. Desire, for one, a drive to reproduce – hence all those stories about faerie children and maidens lost. Hunger for riches is a human thing too, and vengeance is another. Those who live on humans are of course better at acting – and looking – like one.

Knowing what living humans want.

My Pepper-Man claims to have lived mainly on birch trees and ash before he found me. It was through his transformation that I realized how it all had to be. I will tell you more about that later, but for now, let's continue further into the woods.

6

That first time I slipped into the woods with Pepper-Man, I thought it all such a grand adventure. I felt proud to have escaped Mother's punishment and her unfair accusations. I can't recall being afraid at all, though the woods were dark and the destination unclear. I did have faith in my Pepper-Man, though. He walked beside me like a graveyard wraith, his dry hair whipping my face when the wind caught hold of it, his tattered clothes coiling and writhing around his skinny legs. I remember the full moon hanging in the sky, its pale light filtering through the branches. Even though I had known the trees in those woods my whole life, climbed them and picked their leaves, they looked like strangers to me now, draped in darkness and icy light. The path before us – one I ought to know like the back of my own hand – curled like a black snake through the underbrush. Even though I had no reason to think so, I sensed somewhere deep inside that it would lead me to places unknown.

And it did. Or it forked. And suddenly *my* path was no more.

The shift was subtle, like the beginning of a rainstorm with oncoming mist. *My* trees gave way to strange ones, taller and wider, older by far, thick roots curling at their trunks. Their branches brushed my head as we walked beneath them, felt like fingers with very long nails. The path beneath my feet shone dimly in the faint light, scattered with fist-sized leaves; it was like walking on glass or silver, or on a frozen stream. Toads appeared on the path, singing toad songs, loud and croaking. They scattered as we passed through, jumping in among the ferns. An owl hooted somewhere nearby, and I squeezed Pepper-Man's hand when the bird suddenly appeared in front of me, large wings chasing the air. Its eyes shone when it looked at me, just for a second, before it flew away.

'Nothing in here will hurt you,' Pepper-Man said.

'Where am I, then?'

'Visiting with friends.'

'Are they like you?' I felt my heart racing.

'Not at all,' he replied, and then he laughed. It was a hollow sound, that laughter, dry as a husk and dead as winter.

'Where are you taking me?' I tried again.

'Somewhere you are safe, by brook and birch, deep in the stones—'

'Where is that?'

'In the mound. Where I come from – you will see.'

'Are there other girls there?' My heart was fluttering with hope.

'No,' Pepper-Man said. 'You are the only one.'

We walked for what felt like hours, the landscape around us changed again, the air smelled like water-drenched moss, a hint of iron and Pepper-Man. Beneath my naked feet, the ground turned soggy and moist; the trees were drooping shapes with clusters of leaves brushing the ground. I slipped on wet soil and mushrooms, large red toadstools and bigger brown ones that split open when I stepped on them, emitting clouds of spores. The toads were still there, behind us now, like a train of noisy followers. There were slugs, too, and a viper. I could see black bird shapes in the trees; none of them made a sound. The wind was all gone now. The air was quiet but for the toads' throaty voices. I tried not to look at them, kept my gaze trained on the path before us, holding on to my friend, as if his hand were an anchor, safety in the midst of a vast, black sea.

Finally, we came to a halt by a circular shape in the landscape, a grass-covered mound studded with jutting stones.

'Is this it?' I asked, looking up at the towering shape. I could vaguely recall it, from Sunday strolls or maybe just from dreams. 'But how do we get in?' I was yearning for that, getting inside, away from the dark woods, the viper and the toads. I pictured a feast of epic proportions: roughly heaved tables, pigs roasting on spits, like the ones I had read about in my fairytale books.

'It's easy,' Pepper-Man said and pulled me along, and off we went, circling the mound counter-clockwise, one time, two times, three times . . . My feet were beginning to hurt by then, and I fought to keep up with his strides. Twigs and thorny underbrush whipped my calves red and my stomach ached with hunger. Still, I trusted Pepper-Man and felt sure some great reward would follow at the end.

He had said so, hadn't he?

As we completed the third circle, a rumbling sound rose from the ground, and the mound split open like a ripe plum, a gash ran down its side, wet dirt fell in clusters from the edges, and stones and vegetation came tumbling down. I cried out and hid my face against Pepper-Man's body, flinging my arms around his waist.

A chuckle purred deep in his chest, and his hand landed on top of my head.

'Welcome to the mound, little princess,' he said. 'Fear not, but look at the wonders.' I dried tears from my face with the back of my hand, looked up at him, my tall, pale friend, and tried for a tiny smile. 'My tribe is here to welcome you, all the brothers and sisters of the mound.'

They came climbing out of the broken earth then, carrying torches and gifts. Limbs long and thin, hair ragged and braided. Fur and claws, teeth and nails, feather and bones.

The faeries.

First came a tall and spindly woman, carrying a wooden bowl. Her head was bald but for a single white braid, her body shrouded in silk. Her eyes glittered like black jewels; a brown spider spun by her pointed left ear.

'I bring you milk to drink, child,' her soft voice said in my head. She placed the bowl by my feet and took a few steps back.

Next came a man with a long, narrow face. His eyes were slanted and golden brown, his hair a thick mane of red. His clothes, or whatever was left of them, were brown and torn at the seams. A bushy tail hung between his thighs. In his hands, he held a silver tray stacked with soft white cakes.

'I bring you cakes of morning dew,' he said inside my head. His voice was dark, like thunderstorms, his teeth were sharp and very white. The fingernails that touched the tray were curved and very black. He placed the tray at my feet and stepped back.

The next one to approach me had a wreath of wild roses. She was as small as a child, but had the face of a crone. Her dark eyes peered up at me from a wrinkled face, brown as a nut. A roughly woven scarf hid her hair. Her stubby hands held out the wreath to Pepper-Man.

'A crown for our maid,' said the woman, and smiled.

I lifted my gaze, looked at them: a half circle of beings I had never seen the likes of before: tall and small, hairy and bald. Some of them were antlered and others had tails. A few of them were like Pepper-Man, gnarled and tall, some were small, much smaller than I was. All of them looked at me expectantly; animal eyes and human eyes, birds' eyes and blind eyes.

Pepper-Man planted the roses on my head. 'Eat,' he said. 'Drink.'

He lifted the wooden bowl to my lips. The milk was sweet and thick.

He picked a cake from the tray and laid it on my tongue; it melted like sugar when I bit into it, tasted like honey and blueberry jam.

'Now you can enter the mound.' My Pepper-Man laced his hand in mine.

They parted for us when we approached. Smiling faces, glimmering eyes. Hands that patted and touched.

Inviting me into their nest.

Into the dark, dark earth.

Inside, the mound was hollow, as such things are. There was a circular hall with smoking hearths; white stones paved the floor. Torches set in sconces in the dirt wall emitted circles of dirty light. There was a woman there with glowing eyes, playing a wild rhythm on a drum of hide. Birds' feathers stuck out of the ragged clusters of brown hair that hung around her face. She was completely naked and her breasts were milky white. My cheeks reddened and I looked away, unaccustomed as I was to things like that. Her golden gaze followed me as I stepped into the hall, clinging to Pepper-Man's hand. A man in a wig like a French duke spun out in front of my vision; in his hand was a flute of yellowing bone. He lifted it to his lips and played a shrill tune, falling in with the drum. I watched him as he danced away, the frayed brocade of his waistcoat, the faded blue silk of his trousers.

'Dance with me, Cassandra,' said Pepper-Man, grabbing my free hand with his, spinning me slowly around. 'Later we will have more cake, but for now, let us be merry.'

The rest of the party was pooling in behind us, to that dank, hot cave in the earth. One by one, they fell into the dance, moving their bodies in swirls and steps. Swaying and turning, tossing and shaking.

We danced too, spun and flowed across the crowded room, and wherever we went, the others parted for us. Pepper-Man led me with sure steps, lips curled into a lopsided smile. Danced, until there was nothing but the dance. Nothing but the night and the heat, the rhythm and the flesh. Pepper-Man lifted me high up in the air, spun me around, above the crowd. I looked down at the writhing mass of bodies, the horned and the antlered, the feathered and the furred, and I lifted my hands to the cavern's dark roof and let the music take me.

***

I certainly didn't know then that by drinking that milk and eating that cake, I had allowed them all into my life. Not a day went by after that without a faerie peeking its head from the bushes or staring back at me from the mirror when I tried to untangle the knots in my hair. It wasn't just Pepper-Man anymore – although I certainly belonged to him; there were others, too, meddling and distracting. Some I liked, others not. Most were just there at the edge of my vision, dancing, laughing, snarling, and snapping.

'They wish they had a girl like you for themselves,' said Pepper-Man when I complained about them. 'Who would *not* want such a sweet princess with such long, thick hair perched on their knee?'

'I think they look angry, not wishful at all.'

'Trust me, Cassandra – they only want you for themselves. They want to suck you dry as it is, all that golden light right down their throats. That is why the woods are so dangerous for girls such as yourself, you never know what creature of ill intent is lurking. Some of my brothers keep girls' braids in their belts for show.'

'Not you, though.'

'Not I – I only need my Cassandra, and I will protect you, always, from the dangers of the woods. They may snarl and they may snap, but they will never taste my princess.'

Only he did that: taste me – but he liked to show me off. It made me feel special, the way he treated me, the gifts and the kindness, the secrets we shared. The kisses and words that told me he cared. I almost forgot about the pain sometimes, floating on his words.

When he pushed those soft, sweet cakes between my lips, I almost forgot that it hurt.

7

'Have you ever thought about the possibility that you might remember these things wrong?' Dr Martin once asked me.

'I remember them as they were,' I said, crossing my arms over my chest. I was still new then, and unused to our sessions. The chair in his office was large and soft; I often felt like I was drowning in it. My feet didn't reach the floor. I think the chair was meant to comfort us, the strange and troubled youths who went there, but to me it only felt intimidating, as if sitting in that chair meant to lose control. I gave up all hope when that chair grabbed hold and held me captive in its soft lap.

There was an oaken desk in there, but Dr Martin never remained behind it while we talked. He was sitting before me in a more sensible leather chair, his notebook balancing on his knee, pen bleeding blue through the neatly printed lines. His chin was covered in stubble, his hair gray and wispy. His eyes were kind enough, though, when he looked at me.

'Sometimes' – Dr Martin was looking into my eyes – 'something happens that is so horrible, so painful and confusing, our brains take charge and rewrite.'

'I don't know what you mean by that.'

'Let's say someone hit you, someone you trust. Maybe the memory of that incident is so hard to carry that you pretend that it was someone else who delivered the blow – or you don't remember getting hurt at all . . . The mind is a funny thing, you won't believe the things it can do if given the chance—'

'I know you don't believe that Pepper-Man is real.' I looked down at my black shoes, the white stockings. 'None of you do. My mother in particular.'

'It's hard to believe in something you cannot see.' Dr Martin used his patient voice.

'Doesn't mean it's not there.'

'Doesn't mean it is – even if you think so.'

'Are you calling me a liar?' I shifted as well as I could on the soft seat.

'I think you are an editor. I think you have learned to rewrite certain parts of your story, and I suspect there is another truth to the tale.'

'You are wrong,' I told him. 'Everything I tell you is the truth.'

***

I had first met Dr Martin after a long and grueling summer where puberty had hit me, hard and cruel. Mother and I fought over the smallest things, and the china plates often went spinning through the room. She had threatened to send me to a 'special doctor' for years – threatened so often that I ceased to believe it would ever happen, but I suppose the flood of hormones was the last straw. Those I take no blame for; it's just nature, such as it is. But it made everything worse. Worse by far.

I would think back on this time of ceaseless fighting later, when *I* was the one who had to fight – in vain – to make a teenage girl see reason. It's as hard as catching a slick fish, the way she skitters and twirls out of reach.

I guess it made me understand my mother a little better, how our quarrels could drive her to tears and wine. Unlike my mother, though, I didn't have the money yet to pay for someone else to handle the problem. No, I had to deal with my daughter on my own, and not even a barrel of wine would have been enough to take the edge off my misery.

Young girls will do that to you. They will drive you mad.

***

You know very little about your cousin, I suppose. The subject would have made your mother uncomfortable, and Olivia never liked to discuss uncomfortable things. If she *did* speak of it, she would doubtless blame me and call me a bad mother, amongst other unpleasant things. At least I always strive to keep my girl happy and safe, which is something our family has never been any good at.

Your mother has doubtlessly told you the stories about me. How I got into fights at school and enacted strange rituals at home – how people were afraid of me. After the death of Tommy Tipp, I know these stories flared to life again.

Strange how people never forget the wounds inflicted in their childhood.

Even before I met Dr Martin, Pepper-Man had left very little room for anyone else in my life; I had no friends, no playmates or confidantes. Even when he wasn't present, Pepper-Man was there, coloring my world in twilight shades. His world was a dangerous place for a little girl, violent and cruel despite all its wonders. Faeries are no fit company for the living; touching them taints you like a disease. I grew like a pale fruit in the shadows, small and bitter, never getting enough sun – but I grew. I didn't shrivel up and die; didn't fall from the branch and crash to the ground. I was a white apple, a moon-colored pear, a toxic green plum the size of a coin. Grew strange and crooked, but there was life, flushing my veins with rich red blood, enough to sustain more than one.

Olivia, though, she was a child of summer, golden wheat and heavy blossoms. Her birthdays were always splendid affairs. On her tenth, my mother and Fabia set the table in the garden. White tablecloths and vases filled with flowers adorned the large table beneath the oaks. Because Olivia loved it, Mother had brought out the best china: the one with painted pink roses and tender golden rims, each plate accompanied by a small silver fork. Olivia and her gaggle of friends would use them to dismember the strawberry cake, sponge and jam, whipped cream and berries, and ply their soft, round mouths with the mess. Not me, though. No cake for me.

Mother had tried at first, tried to convince Olivia her sister had a natural place at the table, but Olivia would hear nothing of it. She said I was a nuisance. I made her friends uncomfortable. She said they were afraid of me, those braided, frilly girls.

'Cassie will ruin everything,' she told Mother. 'She always does.'

My mother, as always, was not hard to convince. Olivia usually had her way with her, being the golden child. And maybe – just maybe – Mother found it more convenient too, to keep me away from the party. Maybe – just maybe – she worried that the girls would go home afterward and tell their parents what I'd done, if I'd laughed out loud at nothing or whispered to the air. They were afraid of me, sure, but we didn't have many lunatics in S——, and the fear was often mingled with a wicked fascination.

They liked talking about me – a lot.

'You don't want to sit at the table with all those little girls,' Mother told me. 'You're a young woman now, and Olivia and her friends are just children. You wouldn't enjoy it much.'

And she was right, of course, but that was beside the point.

So there I was, rejected, high up in the apple tree with Pepper-Man. I remember I sat on a thick branch, legs straddling the wood. I picked leaves and ripped them in half between my fingers, smelled the strong fragrance as the greenery came apart, then let the pieces fall to the ground. I could see the party between the branches. See the decorated table, the girls clad in white, pink, and blue, fluffy bows tied at their necks, hairbands in their hair. I wore a dress too, but mine was checked in shades of red. Red and angry – like my heart. Pepper-Man sat on a branch above me; his feet made circles in the air.

'You can have the best cake at the mound,' he said, 'sweeter and softer by far.'

'I don't want the stupid cake.'

'Whatever you want, then. Just tell me what you want and you will have it.'

'She does look like a princess, doesn't she?' I was looking at my sister, seated at the end of the table, wearing a new blue dress. Her red braids shone in the sunlight. Father was down there too, taking pictures of the assembly. Ferdinand, banished from the girlish event, slunk behind the flowerbeds and dismantled a yellow tulip with his fingers. Fabia was blowing up balloons.

'What sort of a princess is that, truly?' Pepper-Man shifted on his branch. 'A lonely girl trapped in a gilded cage? Better to be free, like you are, free to be a princess of the mound.'

'I don't want anything of Olivia's,' I said – lied.

'She will be a miserable adult,' Pepper-Man mused, and was absolutely right, as you both well know.

'I bet that cake is good, though.' It was all very confusing. I loathed her and all she had, and yet . . . I leaned forth on my branch to get a better view; listened to the happy girls' chatter that filled the air. 'Smile,' my father rumbled as he aimed the camera. Olivia cocked her head and grinned at him, lifted her braids from her shoulders to let them fall down her chest. Wanted them to be visible in her birthday pictures.

It was then that I saw a shadow creeping slowly across the lawn, shaped much like a slug, with a gaping maw and lantern eyes. The sight of it made my entire body go ice-cold. Though I'd already seen a lot in my life, I had never seen something quite so vile. My grip on the tree branch tightened as it slowly moved toward the party, aiming for Olivia's chair.

'Pepper-Man, what is that?'

I heard him shift above me. 'Cousin,' he sighed. 'That is a cousin of mine.'

'But what is it doing here?'

Pepper-Man paused before answering. 'They do like little girls, especially the happy ones. Happy little girls are like cake to them; like wine and sweet herbs, sugar from a china bowl. It must have heard them laughing in the woods, and now it is here, hunting.'

'That is not good.' I was genuinely concerned all of a sudden. 'Can't you chase it away?'

'It will not listen even if I speak. I would not have either, if someone wanted to keep me from you.'

The girls laughed and hugged each other while grinning at Father's camera. I shifted uneasy on the branch, could hear the sound of my own heart thumping loudly in my chest.

'Your cousin can find another girl to snack on. One of us sisters being food for faerie is more than enough, don't you think?'

'Why this sudden need to protect her?' Pepper-Man's voice was puzzled. 'I thought you loathed Olivia and wished for her to share your fate.'

'No.' I'd rather she remained her own snotty, happy self.

'What do you want to do, then?'

'I want her to be unburdened.' The threat to her had awakened something: a strange and unfamiliar need to nurture and protect. 'We were friends once. We used to be the same, once upon a time.'

'No.' Pepper-Man spoke in a soft voice. 'You never were the same, but I will help you.'

***

That was why I was in Olivia's room that night. In that other white bedroom, a neat and uncluttered twin of mine. That was why I stood there on the white carpet, holding Mother's scissors in my hands. They were ugly, those scissors, big and shiny. Mother used them to cut fabrics. They were the sharpest ones we had.

Olivia was sleeping soundly, head on a lace-edged pillow. She was full of cake and lemonade, and never expected to be visited in her bed.

I approached as quietly as I could, and silently thanked Mother for the thick white carpet that swallowed all sounds. I listened to Olivia's sweet breath; the quiet sighs she emitted in her sleep. Wondered what she dreamt of, the tangerine-marzipan girl, who'd so rudely been targeted by a devourer of happiness. Did she have bad dreams, dark and dangerous, or did she still dream about sunshine and strawberry cake?

When I was quite done looking at her, I carefully lifted her braids off the pillow and held them in my hand, silky and red, thick and heavy, then I took Mother's scissors and snipped them both off. It was very easy; the blades cut through the hair like a silver spade in cake. The braids loosened from her scalp and hung like dead snakes from my palm.

'Come,' Pepper-Man said from the doorway. 'Dawn will be here soon. If we are to complete the ritual, we must hurry.'

'Sure,' I whispered and gave Olivia's sleeping form a last, lingering look. She was still sleeping soundly, hadn't been disturbed at all. I was good at being stealthy. I still am.

Pepper-Man and I tiptoed down the stairs to the living room, where I disposed of the scissors behind an embroidered pillow on the couch. I got the matches from the mantle above the fireplace and borrowed a crystal bowl from a side table. Then Pepper-Man and I went outside through the patio doors, out into the garden. The table out there was cleared by then, no china plates or silver forks were left. A piece of gift wrapping was the only evidence of the party, clinging to the base of an oak's wide trunk. I placed the crystal bowl on the ground and put Olivia's braids in it. Pepper-Man sprinkled the hair with herbs.

'Are you sure this will work?' I asked, hoping I hadn't scalped my sister for nothing.

'It will,' he assured me.

I struggled to light a match in the damp night. Pepper-Man finally helped me, took the matches from my hands and easily lit one. The match sputtered and spat, then it burned with a steady yellow flame. I don't know what Pepper-Man sprinkled on the hair, but it all flamed up like old hay, twisting in the fire, emitting an acrid scent. When the fire died and there was nothing in the bowl but ashes, we brought the bowl with us back inside, up the stairs, and into Olivia's room. She was still sleeping soundly, snoring softly, not knowing that her lovely braids were gone. Following Pepper-Man's instructions, I scattered the bed with the ashes – a drizzle of gray on the starched white cotton – and let out a heartfelt breath of relief.

I looked to Pepper-Man. 'Is she safe now?'

'Yes,' he whispered inside my head.

'She should thank me, then,' I whispered. 'But I don't think that she will.'

'No.' Pepper-Man sounded amused. 'I dare say she won't – not at all.'

***

I was confined to my room after that, of course. Imprisoned within those white walls. The door was not locked but I was strictly forbidden to leave. I didn't cry and I wasn't angry. I just sat in my bed and drew pictures of me and Pepper-Man dancing in the woods or swimming in the brook. Sometimes I stood by the window and watched the feathered faerie who was building a nest in our apple tree. She looked very exotic, all green and red. She had been feeding from an escaped parrot, or so Pepper-Man told me.

On my second day in captivity, I heard a soft knocking on my door. When I opened it, there was no one there, but a white cardboard box lay on the floor in the hallway. When I opened it up, there were cupcakes inside; soft and glossy with frosting. Chocolate and caramel, both my favorite kinds.

I heard my father's heavy steps walking down the stairs. The sharp scent of his cologne lingered.

8

Some girls take on a sort of crystalline quality as they near puberty; caught in that in-between place between child and adult. It's the same quality that so entices the Humbert Humberts of this world. We don't belong to our bodies – our skins. We either float somewhere high above, or are lost in a passion we don't know; a stranger shown up at our doorstep, seducing us with fiery steps and unknown possibilities. We would like to dance that dance. We are terrified of it. We are little lambs and wicked lions.

We don't know what to do with ourselves.

For me, the disconnection from my family had never been more acute. I hated my mother. I hated the children at school. I hated their inability to understand me. I was growing a sense of self that hadn't been there before.

I think I still hated Olivia a little too, even if I had tried to save her. What had she done that I had not, to deserve it all, to be so blessed? We grew up in the same house, in the shadow of the same woods, but only I was haunted. It is hard for a little girl to grasp that fate can be cruel and unpredictable like that. Olivia danced and played in pretty dresses – I bled beneath my Pepper-Man at night.

Sisters, but not really. She held the sun in her chubby little hands; I was left with the moon – ever changing, sometimes black.

'Why me?' I asked Pepper-Man sometimes. 'Why me? Why not Olivia?'

He looked up at me with bloody lips. 'You were here first, and I have grown used to the taste of you now. You let me in, and here I am, forever yours till the end.'

They struck me, those words: I *let* him in. They haunted me for years. How could I possibly have *let* him in? I couldn't recall ever having done anything like that. Was it because I was *wrong*? Was that what allowed him to slip inside?

'And if I told you to leave,' I asked, 'what would you do then?'

'You would never do that.' Pepper-Man gifted me a sharp-toothed smile. 'What would you be then but an angry little girl? It is too late for you now to be like your sister.'

'Because I *let* you in?'

'Because you let me in.'

'And without you I'd be all alone?'

'Who else would stand by your side?'

He was right, of course, my Pepper-Man. Without the secret, I was no one, just an awkward girl whom everyone feared, even my own sister.

He was my best friend, Pepper-Man, the one and only I could count on.

In those dark and painful nights, I felt loved.

***

The summer following Olivia's party, Mother and I fought day and night. My diet was a constant topic of debate: not so much sugar, not so much cream, I would grow fat and curve all wrong. I was already putting on, she said, though I knew she was wrong about that. Whatever I ate, Pepper-Man just sucked the energy right out of me again.

I was a fury of anger and spite; I gorged myself on buttered cookies, drowned my treats in cream. I stole Mother's lipstick and wore it to church. My usual expression was a sneer and I perfected chill in the mirror. I didn't hide my gifts from Pepper-Man anymore, but put them proudly out on display. My room grew into a fearsome wood of twigs and fallen leaves, brilliantly colored feathers, acorns, and sharp rocks.

Mother didn't know what to do with me. She kept eyeing me sideways with a mixture of repulsion and worry in her gaze. She never imagined us growing up, I think. She had only envisioned herself as the mother of toddlers. She had never considered that we would blossom and become adults in our own right, slither from her grasp as we had from her womb, not hers anymore, but belonging to ourselves. Who would she be then, when her son grew a glossy beard and her daughters walked in high heels? No longer the blushing bride, for sure. No longer the young and beautiful mother. Her daughters would knock her off the throne, prettier and more desirable, if only by the grace of youth.

Olivia was caught in the crossfire most of the time. She would crawl up next to our mother and offer soft cheeks of comfort whenever there were tears, perfect pearl-shaped droplets that caught in Mother's lashes. Olivia would be the teddy bear, the sweet child to hug and kiss and make everything feel all right whenever I had been a horror, hurling dinner plates at the walls. I will never forget the looks she gave me, that little tangerine-marzipan girl; dark eyes throwing daggers across the room, accusing me for making our mother sad.

Our brother Ferdinand said nothing while the stoneware flew. He did some half-hearted fencing exercises in the garden, read books on chess and World War I. He was still such a quiet and shy boy, and our shouting gave him headaches. He lay like a pale ghost in bed, cold cloth on his forehead, while Fabia brought him tea on a tray. It wouldn't be long before Mother decided he would do better away from home, and they shipped him off to boarding school, convinced that he would thrive in a more 'wholesome' environment with no mad sister running around.

He didn't, of course. Our brother never did thrive.

My father, like a bear, just watched it all. His eyes were peering from behind folded newspapers, or across the kitchen table where pieces of his rifle were laid out to be cleaned, from behind the hooks of his fishing gear, across the clubs of his golf set, he peered.

Watched.

It was late that summer, after a very long school break, when the last good china plate went crashing to the wall, Mother finally made good on her threat and set up an appointment with Dr Martin.

***

You both know all about Dr Martin, of course, and that book he wrote: *Away with the Fairies: A Study in Trauma-Induced Psychosis*. You might even have read it yourselves. You, Penelope – picking it up at work, perhaps – opening it fearfully while chewing your lunch, choking on tomato wedges and sticky cheese whenever something unpleasant came up. And you, Janus – you really ought to read it, if you haven't already. You would like it, I believe – it would appeal to your analytical mind.

In its pages, Dr Martin recounts our time together since I had first appeared in his office as a scrawny girl of twelve, right up until I married and found no further reason to continue our paid discussions. He also tells me of those in-between years when he was merely my friend, and how he re-entered his role as my psychiatrist after Tommy Tipp died, and witnessed in my defense at the trial.

Your mother came to see me after the book hit the shelves. Pale as a sheet, red hair a mess, Olivia was standing on my porch, clutching at a yellow cashmere shawl haphazardly draped around her shoulders.

'Do you have any idea what you have done?' Her white lips were shivering. 'Mother is a mess. She has taken to bed with a migraine—'

'It's just a book,' I said. 'It's just Dr Martin's words.'

'Why do you hate her so much?' asked my sister. 'Why do you want to destroy our lives?'

I felt a little awkward, seeing her so distressed. Not guilty, mind you, it was never about that. 'No one says it's the truth. I certainly don't believe it's the truth.'

'Then how could you let that doctor say such things?'

'It made him happy, and he was a good friend to me at the trial.'

'You let him publish *lies*! How can you live with that? Have you no love for us at all?'

I shrugged. 'It's just a story. As good as any, I suppose.'

'But people *believe* it, Cassie, can't you see that? He's a professional. A goddamn doctor!'

'People believe what they like.' I considered myself quite the expert.

'Well, you didn't have to endorse his lies. You have ruined us, Cassie, this time for good.'

'According to Dr Martin – my friend – we were already ruined, a long time ago.'

'But those are lies, Cassie. Lies!'

'Oh well,' I said, and shrugged. 'Maybe you're all in denial.'

'Even Father will be cross with you this time, just you see.'

'Father is never cross with me,' I said, but didn't feel so sure. He was always there, watching. Looming like a thundercloud, a dark, uneasy presence.

'You have really outdone yourself with this one,' Olivia went on. 'As if the trial wasn't bad enough. Think about my children, Cassie, they'll never get rid of this smear.'

'They will if they grow up to be strong, confident people. The kind that don't give a rat's ass what people are saying about them.'

Olivia shook her head, a sad expression on her face. 'No one is *that* confident, except for you, perhaps, but then you are stark raving mad.'

'That is a question of perspective.'

Olivia shook her head again, anger and pity flaring in her eyes. 'Not all of us can run off with the fairies, Cassie. Some of us have to stay put and deal with your disasters.'

I laughed then; it was a broken sound. 'Yes,' I said. 'I am sure you wish you were me.'

'That isn't what I meant.' She seemed a little taken aback.

'I know.' I took a few steps closer, forcing her to retreat down the steps. 'I know that isn't what you meant.'

***

Mother may have been in a rage about that book, but I was an adult at the time, and had signed all the appropriate paperwork. I don't believe I cared either way. It was as if that story had nothing to do with me. If it pleased Dr Martin to tell the world his *stories*, he was most welcome to it. I knew a thing or two about *stories*.

Away with the Fairies
A Study in Trauma-Induced Psychosis

Dr V. Martin

Shortly after the murder of her husband, I was summoned by C—'s lawyer to assess her mental state. The lawyer was adamant that her client was too sick to stand trial, and wanted my professional opinion on the matter.

Though I had not been C—'s therapist for years, I was asked due to our long history together and C—'s own trust in me. She was at this point being held in a closed ward at the hospital, having been sent there by the police who observed 'incoherent and disturbing' behavior in her after her husband's body was found.

The psychiatric hospital was a bleak place. The corridors smelled strongly of antiseptics and gravy. C— was there, I think, because they did not know what else to do with her. She was a murder suspect with a history of mental illness, so they could not just leave her to her own devices. She was there for a good six months, both before and during the trial.

I came to see her at least every other day. It was a trying time for both of us. So much time and concern went into C—'s case that I nearly let myself go. I often arrived at the hospital early in the morning only to find that I had forgotten to shave or button up my shirt. We got a room of our own to talk in. Between us was a table of blond wood with a slick surface. The ceiling was so high that even a slight rustling of paper bounced off the walls and came back to us as an echo. Outside the barred windows, the sky seemed very far away. The air inside was stale, despite the humming air conditioner.

My pen spun on the pages of the black notebook as I jotted down our conversations – those words and others would later become the bones and marrow of this very book.

'I do miss him,' C— told me, her fingers caressing a plastic cup of weak tea.

'Of course you do,' I said as gently as I could. 'He was your husband.'

'Not really, though.' She had already told me her own peculiar version of the truth, that her husband had never married her at all. 'I did kill him; T—, I mean, but that was a long, long time ago.'

'You see, we disagree about that. I remember very well meeting you and T— at your house, and he seemed very much alive to me. Very much flesh and blood. Very much a man.'

'He was supposed to appear so,' she said patiently, as if I were a child. 'But it wasn't really real, you know. When the spell finally broke, his body would just be twigs and moss.'

'That is not what the police found in the woods.' I kept my voice calm. 'They found several body parts. All of them were human.'

'It just fell apart, into twigs again.' My patient stubbornly held on to her story.

'That is not what the police saw,' I repeated.

'It was just a residue of the magic. The spell was still powerful enough that it appeared as it should, like a normal human body. Really, it was just twigs. If you opened his casket now, that's all you would find.'

'But you had him cremated, so we cannot do that.'

'That was a mistake . . . I really just wanted the body gone. It was of no use to me anymore – or to Pepper-Man. My husband's heart had run out of fuel.'

'Do you mean he didn't love you anymore?'

'Who? Pepper-Man?' C— looked up from the tabletop.

'No. T—.' I put down my pen and looked her in the eyes.

'T— never loved me,' she protested, again. 'It was just me who was young and naïve enough to think he did.'

'And then Pepper-Man took his place?'

'Yes.'

'You know . . .' I leaned back in the plastic chair and stretched out my legs. 'Could it be that you want to believe that because it is easier to think that you tore up a bunch of twigs rather than a husband of flesh and blood?'

'No. Pepper-Man had been T— for years.'

'Did T— know that?'

'Of course he did – he was Pepper-Man all along.'

'And where is Pepper-Man now?'

'Out in the woods somewhere, with Mara.'

And they haven't come to visit you?'

'No,' she said sadly. 'Not here.'

I decided I would have to push a little harder if I were to readjust C—'s perception of reality. I found the photograph I had hidden between two pages in my book and leaned in across the table. In the photograph was C—, a happy blushing bride, and there was the husband beside her, alive and grinning to the camera. 'I think you did fight in the woods that day. Do you see that?' My fingertip traced the scar that snaked across the groom's temple. 'That could have been from the fall against the rock. Or do you have another explanation for it?'

'If Pepper-Man remembered the cause of T—'s scar, he never told me.'

'I do think you fought,' I continued, 'and then you made up, got married, and lived happily together for twelve whole years.' I pulled the photograph back. 'What changed, C—? Why did you get so mad at him?'

'Nothing changed. The spell just broke. I always knew that it would, eventually.'

'And Pepper-Man, how did he feel about that?'

'It didn't much matter to him. It was just an experiment, being human again. I think he was happy, though, living like that with me. He had friends too, colleagues from work. They drank beer and watched sports on TV.'

'Pepper-Man wasn't always inside T—, though, was he?'

'No. Sometimes he was just himself.'

'Pepper-Man or T—?'

'Pepper-Man.'

'What was T— like then, when Pepper-Man was gone?'

C— shrugged. 'He was nothing, just an empty shell.'

'He did nothing? Said nothing?'

'No, he'd just sit there, empty. Not moving at all.'

'Do you remember a time when T— wasn't Pepper-Man, but just T—?'

'Not since I killed him, no.'

'On that long-ago day in the woods?'

'Yes.'

I sighed and crossed my arms over my chest. 'You do know this story won't do well in court.'

'Well, it's the truth.'

'Can you understand why most people find it hard to believe that a centuries-old fairy animated your husband for twelve years?' I searched her face for traces of deception but found none.

'That is just because they don't know any fairies—'

'And why they would find it even harder to believe that the body in the woods was really just twigs?'

'Well, that is what it was.'

'His family and friends will still believe it was T—.'

'I gave them twelve years extra, didn't I? They believed him to be alive long after he was gone. I spared them the sorrow and grief for a while.'

'Is that so? Then, what would you say to T—'s mother now?'

'That I am sorry the spell failed, but that it is the nature of such things. It can't last forever, at some point it'll give.'

I sighed and almost smiled in my helpless misery. 'I think your lawyer has a very strong case, C—. There is no way they will put you on trial.'

But they did.

9

People loved it, of course. They had all read the newspaper headlines: *Murder Suspect Blames the Fairies!* Who didn't want to know more about that? Get all those tawdry, dirty little details, a peek in under the sheets. Never mind that the court cleared my name, or that a scrawny little woman like me could never have torn her husband's limbs apart like that, not even with a cleaver and an axe.

Away with the Fairies: A Study in Trauma-Induced Psychosis remains to this day *a compelling study of the long-term consequences of childhood abuse.* It's a *strong and personal narrative detailing the patient–doctor relationship between a troubled young girl and a pioneer in his field,* or so said the reviews.

It's all so very easy in Dr Martin's telling; the truth is neatly gift wrapped with a shiny little bow on top. In *his* truth, faerie cakes become pills to drug me, faerie milk becomes alcohol to make me compliant and unresisting. The gifts Pepper-Man brought me were turned into sweets to bribe me with – to pay for my obedience, and my silence.

In his book, Dr Martin wrote about that night I've mentioned – the night when Mother and Fabia went through my room and threw all of Pepper-Man's gifts away. He wrote that it was only cakes, caramels and cupcakes they pulled forth from the nooks and crannies of my room, not crowns of twigs and eyeballs. I can't pinpoint the exact moment of this trans-formation from wood and bone to sugar and frosting, but we had talked a lot, Dr Martin and I, and it could have happened anytime. Maybe it was due to the gifts themselves, enchanted as they were, that their nature changed in the eyes – or ears – of the beholder? Maybe, when I had said 'eyeball', Dr Martin heard 'caramel'; when I said 'hawthorn', he heard 'cupcake'?

Maybe candy was what he expected, so candy was what he got?

It was Dr Martin's way of dealing with the faeries, I think, to break it all down to ingestible bites – something he could chew on and swallow. I ought to be mad, of course, but it's not easy to face a reality like mine. I can't entirely blame him for wanting to create a new one more to his liking.

But Dr Martin's book had ripped large holes in the paper curtains of respectability and normalcy my mother had so strived to keep, despite all my 'afflictions', and even after the horror of my trial. She would never forgive him for that.

I, on the other hand, admired him, for being so bold that he told his truth. That first edition of his book was pink, and so I have insisted that all my novels are too, to honor the late doctor's memory.

In addition, a large percentage of the money from his book sales went to me, to 'the Cassie fund', as Dr Martin called it, knowing very well that my family would likely cut me off, and what was I to do, already without Tommy's income? I lived long and well on that money, it pulled me through until I started making money of my own.

Dr Martin was a very good friend to me.

'In many ways, your mother's delusions run as deep as your own,' he told me once. 'She has made herself blind to the things she will not see, especially the things that can somehow direct blame in her direction.'

It was shortly after the trial, and we were sitting outside a small café, overlooking the ocean, sipping coffee white with cream. Seagulls were soaring high above us; faeries with gills and silvery fish tails were writhing down by the tideline, hair matted with beach sand.

'It's not her fault,' I said, sipping my coffee, pushing the sunglasses further up my nose. I remember it was a blazingly hot day, almost as warm as the day I met Tommy Tipp. It was better by the sea, where a salty draft cooled our skin. I was dressed all in white, innocent as a dove.

'Well,' he replied, measuring me with those intense, brown eyes. 'It certainly isn't *your* fault either. You have been let down in so many ways,' he said, wiping his brow with a handkerchief, popping a capsule for his heart. He was a very old man at that point; his practice had closed and he spent his senior years writing – about me.

'What you said before, in your draft,' I was referring to the still unfinished manuscript that he'd graciously let me read, 'that we will never truly know what happened to me, but that someone, somewhere, knows the truth . . .'

'Yes?'

'Were you thinking of my mother then?'

'I was.'

'But if she is delusional as well, maybe her truth will be as twisted as mine, compared to *your* beliefs.'

'That might very well be. But that's why I write this book. It's all for you, Cassie – in your defense. Someone ought to tell it like it is, even if your mother can't or won't. To *redeem* you.'

'It's a little ironic that Mother was the one who called you in the first place, way back then.'

'To have someone take the problem off her hands, no doubt.'

'Would she really have done that if she was in on some big, dark secret?'

'Denial, my dear,' Dr Martin said. 'Denial is a powerful drive.'

'Mara says that *you* are the one in denial, and that she will leave a token on your pillow tonight to prove it.'

'Oh, please, no.' The old man's face fell in stubbly, fleshy folds. 'Please tell her not to. I would hate for my wife to find you squabbling around our house at night.'

'Mara will. I will stay at home.'

'Of course you will.' A twinkle in his eyes.

'Just you see.' I left it at that.

Mara said later that she had indeed visited the doctor that night, leaving half a leaf and an acorn by his side. Dr Martin never mentioned it, though, so either he had not seen it, his wife had picked it up, or he thought it was something the cat dragged in.

Or maybe – just maybe – he too was in denial.

***

Despite our different opinions, he was a good friend to me, Dr Martin. Without him, I might not have escaped those first tribulations quite as unscathed, even if it was technicalities more than anything else that sealed the outcome of the trial. It was still nice of him to try to *redeem* me.

He was dead by the time those other deaths took place, and I still often wonder what he would have made of those.

10

I remember, a long, long time ago, when I first told Pepper-Man about seeing Dr Martin. We were lying in our meadow at the edge of the woods; it was a warm night, but twilight was settling. It was our favorite time of the day, that silent hour before night arrived. Our chosen spot was so peaceful, no strollers or dog walkers ever went there. I suppose that was due to Pepper-Man; his presence felt unsettling to most people. When I lay on my back and looked up, I could see the treetops swaying, the birds rushing across the sky. He held my hand. It had changed over the years. Where he used to look gnarled, he was smooth. Where he used to be pale, he held a soft, pink pallor. His warts were gone; his lips were red. His white, white hair had turned to silk. It was my doing, I know that now, it was due to my blood, which sustained him.

He was becoming more like me.

'What if the doctor thinks I'm mad?' I squeezed his fingers. 'What if he locks me up somewhere?'

'I would find you.' Pepper-Man squeezed my fingers in return. His eyes didn't look so murky anymore, but had become a deep and warm forest green.

'Would you break me out of the asylum?' I was only half joking.

'I would break you out no matter where you were kept. Do you recall the night of the first feast? I came for you then.'

'That is true,' I admitted.

'Nothing they can do to you is important. All that is important is here, between us.'

'Mother would disagree.'

'*Mother* does not know you.'

'But you do?'

'I do.' He turned over so he lay on his side, looking down at me, head resting in his hand. His tattered rags were gone by then, replaced by clothes of charcoal gray. 'Here.' He handed me a mason jar that I recognized from our pantry. The orange spread it used to contain was gone; instead there was a sprig with two black berries, a dead white butterfly, and four dry pine needles inside.

'What is this?' I looked at the curious contents.

'What you wished for, my Cassandra. It is a story for you to tell people – something they will believe.'

He was right, I had said that. I shook the jar gently. 'A story, huh?'

'Indeed. You might enjoy that more than crowns now, maybe.'

'You mean I have outgrown your necklaces and rings?'

'A little.' Pepper-Man smiled. Despite his new beauty, the smile still looked cruel; his teeth were too sharp and his lips too red.

'How do I get it out?' I turned the jar over.

'Boil it in water and drink it as tea, or you could eat it as it is, from the jar.'

'Water it is, then.'

Pepper-Man sat up on his knees and lifted my skirt away from my thighs, searched with his finger for an unmarked patch of flesh.

'Do not fret about the doctor,' he said before his head dipped down to feed. 'Nothing *they* can do can ever hurt you.'

***

Faerie gifts can be many things. Sometimes they come as inspiration. Trinkets and baubles and crowns I can go without, but I find myself addicted to the faerie tea; liquid stories delivered in jars. There is nothing like the feeling of its power unfurling inside, petal by petal – a fresh story. Faerie magic is the purest kind of magic, blending nature skillfully. Faeries know everything that lives around them, are drawn to life – and death – itself. They feel the essence of every bone and every tree. In my jars, an angry spruce and a melancholy willow meet a burst of happy buttercups, or the bitter decay of a dead wasp. No one knows quite how the stories will turn out, not even the faerie who makes them. That's a part of their alchemy – to never quite know the outcome. It makes it as interesting for them as for me, to see how a particular blend will turn out. Faerie magic is fickle magic: there are no guarantees.

He knew what he did, Pepper-Man, on that late and lazy summer's day, he bound me with powerful shackles. He was always good at that, my friend, finding new ways to please me. New gifts to dazzle me with, new chains to bind me. Was in me, always, tooth and claw.

There is no escape from Faerie.

***

Those faerie gifts did save me; they made my miserable life feel worthwhile. Though I loathed my mother's house and the walls of the white room, at least I had an escape. Between the enchanted stories and my Pepper-Man, I felt like I could breathe. For years, it was all I had: Pepper-Man, those jars – and Dr Martin.

***

That idea of escape – that desperation – is why I threw all my caution overboard, I think, when Tommy Tipp came along. Golden of hair, blue of eyes. I so desperately wanted to be saved then, for someone to show me the way out.

I wasn't so much enticed by the idea of love as such, even back then it never rang true to me.

'True love'. 'Meant to be'.

None of that meant anything to me. Smelled like a lie – it still does. It's just another one of those things you ought to have in order to build your life right. It's a screen to hide behind.

If you have a husband, you cannot truly be that bad.

If your husband is handsome and capable too, more glitter falls on you. If you don't have it, you are deemed unworthy, different and possibly *wrong*. Without the love of a good man – any man – you are spoiled fruit, lacking an essential stamp of approval. Never mind if you are ill suited for it and would've been much better off alone. Never mind if your inclinations are such that living with another human being is difficult and even harmful. Live with another you must, or face eternal shame and disgrace. Forever be second-class. No stamp of approval for you.

I didn't think much about such things when I met Tommy Tipp, though, and started sleeping with him in the woods. I figured we could move in together when autumn arrived and the forest floor became cold and wet. It was best suited for summer nights; soft moss and scented air.

The faeries gathered all around us; laughing, pointing and waving.

I didn't care if they saw. My heart was a mess. I was unaccustomed to that as well; that flutter and that ache, the honey that poured forth whenever he was near, sticky and golden, coating everything in sweetness.

Pepper-Man said that I even tasted like honey, spicy and warm, in those early Tommy-days.

11

And now, my young friends, it's finally time to talk about Tommy Tipp and what happened to him in those woods.

***

That summer we met, Tommy, though twenty-four, was still living with his parents. Things had been a bit hard for him after the release from prison, and he had problems moving on. His mother was a gray and bitter woman who sold buttons and ribbons and threads for a living. His father repaired cars.

I was eighteen when I met him, working part-time at the library, trying to find my footing in a world that hadn't treated me kindly. I was contemplating college; sipped tea from mason jars and wrote every night, with Pepper-Man reading over my shoulder. Mother and Dr Martin were feeding me pills: an array of blue, white, and purple dots. I always spat them out; flushed them down the toilet. Pepper-Man said they weren't good for me; incompatible with faerie food. I, of course, was living at home too, my white room filled with dead greenery feeling smaller and more oppressive by the day.

***

Tommy thought I was peculiar, *different*. That was what drew him to me. I wasn't like the other women swooning at his feet. To be honest, I hadn't thought of men much at all at that point. I had Pepper-Man, Mara, and my friends in the woods, how could there be room for more? I also knew that I was broken. I knew that the life I led set me apart, and that there would never, ever, be a bridging of that gap – but Tommy was different too. He was living on the fringe of things, just as I did, only on another fringe. He would never wholly be part of the establishment in S—, his past would always be with him, his reputation would always condemn him – he too was broken in the eyes of the world. That, I think, was why I let him in.

We all know now that it was a mistake.

He had approached me at work when he came in to read the newspapers and scan the job ads, or pretend to, anyway. I think the lack of attention I paid him, pushing my trolley, sorting through books, annoyed him no end. He was used to being looked at, his self-esteem depended on it. He knew all about *me*, of course. Knew I was Olivia Thorn's half-mad sister who used to walk alone in the woods, talk to invisible people, and sometimes even throw things in anger. That didn't faze him at all.

One day he came over while I was at the desk and leaned in on the wooden counter:

'Are you as crazy as they say?' His blue gaze burrowed into mine.

'Yes.' I stifled a smile. 'Crazier,' I said.

'Good,' he replied, combed through his hair with his hand. Seemed a little nervous. 'Do you want to go for a walk when you're done? Have an ice cream?'

'Why?' I asked.

'Because it's a hot day, and ice cream is better with company.' He tried to dazzle me with a smile, but it fell a little flat. I was puzzled more than anything else. I didn't understand what he wanted.

'Why?' I asked again.

'Because sweetness is better shared,' he replied and added a wink. I didn't get it. Shook my head in confusion.

He sighed. Fidgeted. 'Look, I just want to get to know you, that's all. I see you all the time in here, pushing that trolley around . . . I just thought you seemed lonely, that's all. Wondered if you'd like some company.'

I swallowed hard. No one had approached me in that way before, and he did seem sincere. Old warnings about going with strange men flashed through my mind, but of course I didn't heed them. I was never afraid of the same things that other girls were afraid of. Had no reason to be. I was always well protected from strangers.

'All right,' I said at last, and watched his shoulders relax as he let out his breath. He rarely had to work for a yes, so my reluctance must have been hard to swallow.

He waited for me then, when I got off work; leather jacket thrown over his shoulder, to show off his abs no doubt, and the sculpted chest under his shirt, but I didn't care about things like that. We slowly made our way down to the pier, where the ice cream parlors lay scattered like colorful beads, sporting small tables under plastic parasols. I remember a gentle breeze spinning candy wrappers and newspaper pages on the ground, the unfamiliar sensation of walking side by side with a man. Remember that I didn't know what to say, didn't know how to act, and how that bothered me.

Tommy Tipp wasn't tied for words, though.

'Who are you talking to?' he asked, when we sat by a white plastic table licking at our ice cream cones. 'When you are talking to yourself,' he clarified. The sun was really blazing that day, licking his hair with gold. The pink ice cream melted faster than I could eat it, fat droplets ran down the sides, curling across my fingers, aiming for my wrist.

'My invisible friends,' I said, not really trying to be coy. Flirting was a foreign language to me, in which *he* was fluent, of course.

'Oh, really.' His eyes twinkled. 'What do they have to say that is so interesting?'

'They tell me things,' I replied, still honest. Found no reason to lie, even if I knew Mother wanted me to.

'What do they say, then?' He urged me on; he had an expression on his face that I didn't understand, a little teasing, a little taunting.

'All kinds of things.' I shrugged.

'Do they tell you about hidden treasures, or who is kissing who?'

'No.' Sometimes they did, but that was hardly the point.

'What do they tell you, then?'

'Normal things. Everyday things. Although it is mostly just one. A "he".' I didn't mention Mara then, she was precious to me and secret, even more so than Pepper-Man.

'Really?' Tommy seemed intrigued by the mention of my faerie companion. 'Is he your boyfriend?'

'Not really.'

'Is he a ghost?'

'Perhaps . . .'

'Would he be jealous if you found yourself a *real* man?'

'Maybe,' I replied honestly. I really didn't know how Pepper-Man would react. 'He *does* think of me as his.'

'Is that a challenge?' Tommy grinned widely behind the remains of his ice cream, a droplet of pink on his chin.

I shrugged, finally falling into that soft playfulness, that sweet, sweet prelude to love.

Tommy looked at me, still smiling. 'Challenge accepted,' he laughed, and winked.

'It might not be pretty,' I warned him, having caught sight of Gwen, a golden-furred faerie I knew, by the ice cream parlor's counter. She was looking straight at me, shaking her head while her white-tipped tail swept the floor behind her.

'I am used to hard bargains,' said Tommy Tipp, crumpling the paper napkin in his hand. 'No doubt you know all about me already.'

'Only what they say, and they do say a lot of things.'

He laughed at that, tussled his hair with strong fingers. 'They don't know the half of it, and what they *do* know, they got wrong.'

'Tell me, then,' I urged him, found myself increasingly taken with his eyes. They were the bluest blue I had ever seen. All kinds of light lived in there.

Gwen was approaching me while we spoke. When she was close enough, she bent down and whispered in my ear, 'Don't be a fool, little Cassie. Your husband will not stand for it.' I felt confused then, for a moment. Pepper-Man was not my husband, was he? I decided to ignore Gwen, although it was hard; she smelled like the fox she fed from, a rank odor of fur and wilderness, mixed with a hint of old blood.

'I wanted a different life, you know,' Tommy Tipp told me across the table. 'I just wanted adventure, a life that was a little more unpredictable than the one my parents had.'

'Crime can certainly be exciting,' I agreed. 'Or so I suspect, anyway.'

'You have never done anything *wrong*, have you, Cassie?'

'Oh, God, I can't do anything *right*.'

'Wrong in the eyes of the law, I mean.'

'No, no . . . I don't think so.'

Gwen placed a paw at the nape of my neck, pressed hard enough that I could feel her black claws digging into my skin. 'What about your treasure at the mound, Cassie? What about your family?'

I pulled away from her hand, but my head snapped toward the faerie. 'He won't mind,' I told her. 'He won't mind at all. He only wants what is best for me.' I had forgotten to speak silently in my head. I forgot that all the time, but wished I hadn't done it then.

'What? Did you speak to your invisible friend?' Tommy was amused, his eyes were wide with wonder. 'Did you do that just now? Did you speak to him?'

'It isn't him, it's a she,' I admitted. 'And she doesn't want me to talk to you.' I shot Gwen a furious look. *Go away*, I told her silently. *Go away.*

'Why?' Tommy's gaze searched the air where Gwen was standing.

'She thinks he'll be upset – but he won't.' At least I hoped he wouldn't. Pepper-Man didn't always do what I thought he would.

'You don't seem so sure.' A smile tugged at Tommy's lips. 'What do you think he'd do if I kissed you?'

'Nothing, probably. But he *can* be unpleasant.' I flinched as Gwen pinched me.

'You should not talk of him like that,' she said, and I shivered a little, because Gwen was usually so nice to me.

'Unpleasant how?' asked Tommy Tipp.

'It doesn't matter, because he won't be,' I decided. Surely, Pepper-Man would only be thrilled if I found a nice young man to keep me company. He was my best friend, after all – my only champion in this world.

'We ought to find out,' said Tommy.

When we left the ice cream parlor that day, Tommy Tipp held my hand in his as we walked down the pier. There was a flutter in my heart that I'd never known before. His skin was so soft and so warm, his crooked smile, which had seemed so ordinary just hours before, was as if enchanted. Suddenly I could see its dazzling qualities just as clearly as any of his house-wives. He truly was magnificent, I thought, stealing glimpses of him from the crook of my eyes. Truly, very handsome.

And he hadn't laughed at me at all – not like that, cruel and mocking. His peals of laughter had been soft and carefree, and he really did seem to want to know about the faeries, kept asking me about them as we approached the town center.

'How often do you see your invisible friends?'

'Not very often,' I lied. 'A few times a week, perhaps.' I didn't want to overwhelm him. It felt too fragile, that tender bond we were forging. That's why I didn't tell him that Gwen was still with us, just a few steps behind his back, and that other faeries had joined with her, forming a ribbon of ragged bodies, horns and claws, walking in our tracks. I didn't want Tommy to notice, so I didn't look back much, but I could tell that Hawking was there, a tall faerie Pepper-Man's size, with hair just as black as Pepper-Man's was white, and Francis too, a young-looking faerie I always suspected of being a change-ling. Some of the smaller ones were cheeky and nipped at my skirt as I walked. Esteban, with the giant bat wings folded on his back, came up beside me, gave me a smirk:

'I would eat your friend if you were mine.' His dark gaze bore into mine.

'Pepper-Man won't do any such thing.' I was clever this time, and spoke silently in my head.

'He will not stand for it,' Esteban warned, just as Gwen had done.

We all walked up the main street, between store windows displaying dresses and candy. Tommy Tipp still held my hand in his – was telling me about prison; about his cellmate who also saw invisible things. Ghosts, he said. His cellmate saw ghosts.

'Every night at three a.m., he woke up with a start. That's when the guy who died in our cell came back, banging with a spoon on a pan. He used to be a cook, I think, before he went in for murder. I never saw or heard him myself, but my cell-mate swore it was the truth.'

'My visitors aren't like that. They don't follow the clock.'

'But it's basically the same, isn't it?' The faeries sniggered behind us.

'Well,' said I, 'they *are* dead.' Someone kicked my leg.

'I just want you to know that I am open to all kinds of stuff. Maybe you were born a medium?'

'Maybe.' I felt faint. 'Where are we going?'

'I'm walking you home, the long route.' Another one of those dashing smiles. 'You don't mind, do you?'

'No.' How could I resist having his hand in mine as long as I possibly could?

We were almost through the street, up by the church, when he suddenly pulled my hand. 'Come,' he said. 'Let's tempt fate.' A line he had used a lot, I'm sure. We went in through the gate, and walked into the cemetery. Cleverest move he could make, although he didn't know that, of course. Faeries do not like graves and crosses. It reminds them of what they are – what they were. That their natural state is rotting bones. They all remained at the gate.

'Come,' Tommy Tipp said again, and pulled me with him in among the yews. There, beneath the poisonous needles, he closed his arms around me, held me to his warm, living body, and kissed me softly on the lips. Once, twice. Then the kiss turned fierce and hungry, left me a warm and shivering mess. His hands kneaded my back through my dress, and my hands tangled in his hair while we kissed.

I saw him then, over Tommy's shoulder: a lone figure close to the gate. Pepper-Man was staring right at me across the tombstones, hands clenched at his sides, hair lifting in a breeze only he could feel. But he was smiling, yes, he was smiling. I relaxed then, and gave in to the moment, enjoying every kiss I got. Not even worrying for another second that Pepper-Man would eat the man that I already loved.

***

I fell for him like a fool. No reservations, no caution. In Tommy, I thought I had found someone who could shoulder me, carry me and accept me.

I never thought I'd have that.

To him, I was a mystery, I think. A new adventure to embark on – something he couldn't quite figure out. He *did* love a challenge, Tommy Tipp.

We were both very happy at first.

12

Tommy was not a man to share his feelings, but he seemed to like me well enough. He used to wait for me outside the library and would wrap his warm hand around mine as we headed for the woods. I asked him once what he saw in me that the rest of the world failed to see.

'You think more than you look,' he replied, lying on his side, completely naked, teasing my cheek with a straw.

'What does that mean?'

'Well, you don't wear any lipstick, and you read a lot of books.'

'So I am not pretty, then?'

'You are,' he said, and then: 'In a peculiar way.'

'But aren't you embarrassed to be seen with me in town?'

'Why?' His eyebrows rose. 'We are doing them a favor, giving them something to talk about.'

'What about your parents, then, what do they say?'

He shrugged. 'They stopped telling me what to do a long time ago. But what about you, Cassie, aren't you embarrassed to be seen with a no-good criminal like me?'

'I haven't really thought about it.' I was surprised by this shift in perspective. I was so used to being the embarrassing one that it felt strangely thrilling to be on the other side. 'I am not embarrassed. I think I am mostly in love.'

Tommy didn't reply to that, but his cheeks looked flushed

and he smiled. He picked up a straw from the ground and gently tickled my face with it. 'You're a strange one, Cassie,' he said.

We were a good match like that, Tommy and I, both of us stains on our mothers' Sunday bests. Maybe it was only natural that we gravitated toward each other. Where else could we find acceptance like that? Who was better suited to understand the other one's plight than a fellow outcast?

Pepper-Man was supportive of my plan to move out of the white room, but he had little patience with me swooning over Tommy.

'It is an affliction, this hunger and craving. It will pass soon enough, you ought to know that.' We were in the white room, in the white bed, beneath the white sheets.

'Why?' I asked, heady on love.

'Because it is easy to make promises you would rather not keep later on. True companionship, like ours, it lasts, it is sealed by blood and magic. This other companionship, the one you have with him, it is fleeting as a shooting star – magnificent in the moment, but then it is gone. You ought to prepare for that day.'

'Why?'

'Because you must know what to do when he no longer suits you.'

'I will never tire of Tommy Tipp.'

He sighed and rolled over, away from me. 'Of course you will. You will not have time to visit the mound if you build your life with him.'

'I will always have time to visit the mound. Tommy understands. He knows I have other friends that he can't see.'

'True, but he does not truly *understand*.'

That, of course, was true. Tommy knew little about magic and blood. How deep it runs, how strong. 'But you don't mind, do you? That I feel the way I do about Tommy Tipp, and that I sleep with him in the woods—'

'Of course not.' He turned back over, facing me again, green eyes gleaming. 'It is good to see you so happy, my Cassandra – and what is he to me but a puff of air? He will be gone again soon, believe me, I know.'

'I don't think that he will.' I spoke quietly. 'I don't think that I will ever stop loving Tommy Tipp.'

Pepper-Man held my hand. 'I know that you think that, my sweet, but people are not always what they seem.'

***

I have often thought that Pepper-Man knew already then, that Tommy had secrets. That he had watched him and knew the truth, long before I caught on. It was as if he were preparing me for that blow that was to come . . . In hindsight, I don't know how I feel about that, but what I *do* know is that it wouldn't take long before the harsh sting of hate accompanied the honey-love I felt in those first summer days with my Tommy.

***

And here we have arrived at the pearl in the oyster. At that thing you have been aching to know. I will not tease and taunt you any longer, you have been more than patient with me. I will tell you what happened to Tommy Tipp. I will tell you, and then you can judge me as you please.

***

It was at the end of that sweet summer of love.

I hadn't made plans to see Tommy that day, but my heart swelled just by thinking about him. I had finished my day's job at the library, sorting through old editions of crime novels and mystery books. I had decided to go to the mound after work, to see Mara and Pepper-Man, instead of going home. What was I to do at home? Leisure about in that cramped white room, listening to my mother's complaints about my clothes, my hair, and the way that I walked?

My mother had to wear glasses now, silver-rimmed and angular, and it did nothing to soften her appearance when she came at me nagging, red lips a slash on her skin. Her hair was dyed as blond as before, just as neatly curled and stiff. She reminded me of a soaring falcon, always on the lookout for juicy prey; someone who stumbled and fell. My father had let middle age come and do as it pleased, gifting him with white hair and a potbelly. He had let his facial hair grow, possibly at my mother's behest to hide away wrinkles and saggy skin. The full beard made him look more than ever like a wild and angry bear.

Ferdinand at that point was a young man at the brink of adulthood. He was pale and lanky, a silent ghost, invisible between us girls: me, the mad embarrassment, and Olivia, the fledgling beauty queen of S——. Our brother was clever enough to keep a low profile, did well in school and kept to himself when he was home on vacation. Slipped under Mother's radar as a slick fish. I'm not sure what he did with his time. None of us knew, I suppose.

If I have one regret in life, it is my brother.

I was headed to the woods that day, to the mound. I knew the way well by then; knew how to let my world slip away and the ground beneath my feet guide me to the *other* path. It wasn't hard to slip through the veil; walking between the worlds was as easy for me as putting on a pair of gloves.

On that particular day, Pepper-Man came to greet me. He

94

was standing on the path, just by the edge of the woods. A tall, dark-clad sentinel among the towering trees.

He turned his head to me, his expression like carved marble. 'Don't go any further today, Cassandra.'

'Why? Is something amiss?'

'Let us do something else . . . Let us just walk for a while, the other way.'

'No,' I said. 'I want to see Mara.'

Pepper-Man just shook his head, though. 'Mara can wait. You do not want to do this.'

'What?' My heart was hammering wildly in my chest. 'What is it? Why can't I walk to the mound?' I was scared by then. Pepper-Man was rarely stern.

Pepper-Man didn't answer my question; instead he said: 'We can take another path. There are many roads leading to the mound.'

'But why can't we go this way? You *have* to tell me. Has it something to do with Mara, is she all right?'

'Mara is safe. She is in the mound braiding feathers in her hair.'

'What is it, then? *What is it?*'

Pepper-Man took a moment, green eyes measuring me. 'Very well, then, my Cassandra. I will show you.'

I have been thinking about that moment a lot. Especially in these latter years I have been thinking – wondering – how much of the random occurrences that took place around that time were really Pepper-Man's designs. He knew me very well, mind you, knew where to push and prod. And he was ambitious and bold, my Pepper-Man, old and cunning, too.

Maybe he wanted things to end up the way that they did all along.

Pepper-Man brought me further into the woods, but the path didn't fork as it used to when I was walking to the mound. No, it continued straight ahead, to the 'love spot', as I called it in my head, where Tommy Tipp and I used to go to frolic.

'What is it?' I asked my companion's back, the fall of straight, white hair. 'Where are you taking me? Where do we go?'

He didn't answer me straight away but kept warding me off: 'Be patient, my Cassandra.' 'You ought to see for yourself.' And the ominous: 'Remember, my sweet, I did warn you.'

We arrived at the love spot. The bubbling brook behind it rushed with water, and was so loud it drowned out the sounds when we approached. I didn't hear them until I saw them: Tommy Tipp with his jeans around his ankles, and before him on the ground, a woman with her pink top riding across her collarbone, huge, soft breasts jiggling whenever he thrust between her legs. His buttocks looked so scrawny and white, seen from that awkward angle. The woman bit her lip, pine needles caught in her long, brown hair. I could see it was the mother of one of Olivia's friends, an obnoxious girl called Annie. My honey heart instantly spilled over with salt, polluting all the sweetness. It felt like Tommy Tipp had hit me – hard – right at the pit of my stomach. My lips pressed together, my eyes filled with tears. Inside me, a shrieking howl began to build as my castle of dreams shattered.

Pepper-Man's arm draped over my shoulders. 'What do you want to do now?' he whispered inside my head.

I pulled him with me off the path, in among the trees. I didn't want Tommy to see me yet, as if disturbing them in the act made *me* lesser, somehow.

Between the tall trees, I lifted my red skirt over my hips, inviting Pepper-Man inside. A petty and useless revenge, I know, especially since it was only Pepper-Man, but at least it kept me from screaming. I imagined that I heard the other two moaning while Pepper-Man was inside me, but that could just have been me. I was backed up against a tree, legs curled around Pepper-Man's waist. The rough trunk was bruising my backside and my panties on the ground were swarming with ants. When I climaxed, I hoped that was the end of it and that the anger and hurt would leave with the release, but when Pepper-Man lowered me down to my feet, I was still as furious and broken as before.

'What do you want to do now?' he asked again, licking my blood off his lips.

'We wait,' I said, edging closer to the love spot through the greenery. My back ached from the rough tree bark, my thighs were slick with fluids. I left the ant-infested underwear behind on the ground.

Peeking in on the love spot between the branches, I could see that Tommy Tipp was also quite done. He was zipping up his jeans. Annie's mother was hooking her bra back in place. Her face was slack and flushed, she looked sated.

Tommy was standing a little away from her; looking in another direction. Already done with Annie's mother, I thought. He picked up his leather jacket from the ground and fished around in the pockets for his cigarettes – he always did that after. The familiarity of those movements drove daggers into my broken heart. It was him, it was really him – *my Tommy* – who had betrayed me.

I waited until they left the love spot and entered the winding path. Tommy walked first, smoking. She followed in tow, buttoning her shirt. Neither of them spoke to the other. Maybe there was nothing to say.

I stepped onto the path before them, hurt and anger bubbling up.

'How *could you*?!' I asked, my face twisting up when I began to cry.

'Cassie . . .' He came to a halt before me, eyes confused, mouth slack.

'How could you do that to me?' I wailed, deep sobs ripping from my chest.

'But Cassie—' He tried to put a hand on my shoulder, which I briskly brushed away. I took a few steps back, fighting the powerful sobs that kept coming, fueled by rage and disappointment.

'You were supposed to be the one, you were the one who would take me away!'

'I better leave,' said Annie's mother, brushing past us, touching his shoulder lightly with her fingertips. I wanted to smack her. Hard.

'Cassie,' he said again, after she'd left. He placed a hand on each of my shoulders, tried to catch my gaze with his. 'I've never promised you anything.' His eyes were sincere. 'I've never said I'd take you anywhere. We just had some fun, that's all.'

'But I thought we were in love.' My voice was still wailing, snot and tears streamed down my face.

Tommy Tipp laughed. He *laughed*. 'I don't even think you know what that means, Cassie. And even though I like you, I like other women, too.'

He made me feel so stupid then. It hadn't even occurred to

me that he shared that kind of intimacy with someone else. I had taken exclusivity for granted.

'Look,' he said. 'It's not like *you* don't see other guys. I can feel it sometimes, when I'm inside you, that someone has been there, and recently. But you've never heard *me* complain.'

'That's different,' I sobbed, drying my tears with the back of my hand, and then with the hem of my skirt.

'How is that different?' His voice was slightly annoyed. 'And don't give me that talk about your "invisible friends", we both know that's just lies. If you are having a good time, at least you should own up to it.'

'Like you do?' I still held the skirt hem in my hands.

'Like I do,' he replied, and then he saw it all. 'Why are you naked?' He had caught sight of my lack of underwear, the moist trails on my thighs. 'Were you looking at us?' His eyes widened in astonishment. 'Were you *touching* yourself?' His lips split in a wide smile, his laughter rose above the treetops. 'You are really the most twisted person I've ever met, Cassie. Do you know what people like you are called? Perverts.' He spat the word. 'That is what they're called.'

It was then that I hit him.

It happened so fast: a flash and a blur, and maybe – just maybe – an aiding hand coming in from behind me, adding some speed and power to the blow.

Tommy Tipp, taken aback, fell backward into the underbrush, his expression a mixture of surprise and disbelief.

In the underbrush was a stone, half hidden by the ferns, and on the stone was a sharp jutting edge, like a dagger, which Tommy's head hit very hard. It sliced through his temple and into his brain.

I don't believe he suffered much.

But there I was, broken and crushed – a widow before I even got married – looking down at the corpse of Tommy Tipp, his blood a slick pool on the stone.

***

You would be confused at this point, I guess. This all happened long before you were born, yet you have met Tommy Tipp many times. He was my husband for over a decade, so how could he have died at twenty-four? Tommy was not what you thought he was, but then I have told you that already.

If you keep turning the pages, I will tell you just what he was.

13

After Tommy had fallen, Pepper-Man and I stood quiet for a while, just looking at his body draped across the ferns, his head resting on the bloody stone, golden hair matted with red. I felt bereft more than anything else. A shiny dream had been taken from me, and I was left with a problem the size of a well-grown man. Not that I didn't mourn him, mind you, but all of that came later. Right there, right then, it was *bereft* that I felt, mingled and mixed with a drizzle of shock.

'Is he really dead?' I asked my friend, hoping against all odds that there was still a spark of life in there.

'He is.' Pepper-Man's naked toe touched the hem of Tommy's jeans.

'What do we do now?'

'We have to dispose of his remains. It would not do if some stroller came by.'

'Shouldn't we alert someone?'

'Do you *wish* to alert someone?'

'No . . . not if it can be helped.' A fresh fear bloomed in my stomach: I envisioned myself imprisoned for life; saw my mother's furious gaze before my inner-eye and Dr Martin's head shaking with disappointment. No more playing in the woods for me. No more Mara. No more Pepper-Man—

'Not to worry,' said Pepper-Man then. 'My sisters in the brook will take care of him for you.'

'Really?'

'For sure.' And then we got to it.

Pepper-Man took hold of Tommy's torso, pried his head from the stone. I took care of the legs, although Pepper-Man was so strong that my contribution was mostly for show. We carried him across the love spot, and my state of mind was such that I didn't even reflect on the fact until afterward, that my dead lover's body was carried across the same patch of soil that so recently had seen our naked backs and tasted the salts of our passion.

When we came to the brook, we put Tommy down. His mouth was open, jaw slack. His temple was a mess of torn skin and gristle. His blue eyes stared empty out in the air. He wasn't Tommy anymore, was some ragdoll impersonation, empty of essence – of life.

'Will they take him to the mound?' I asked.

'No' – Pepper-Man shook his head – 'this one is not for us.'

'How can you tell?' I could somehow envision it: Tommy turning into a troll, or a ram-horned faerie with cloven feet.

'He is not strong enough to join Faerie.' Pepper-Man's foot was on Tommy's hipbone, ready to push him into the dancing stream.

'Or you don't want him there.' I was suddenly overcome with suspicion.

'If you ask, I do believe you can do better,' Pepper-Man admitted as Tommy went out in the water.

He dipped, but didn't sink; rose to the surface, face down. The stream tugged at his clothes, ready to take him further down – but then the hands came, pale and thin, reaching out of the rushing stream. Seven of them, maybe eight, they grabbed hold of the body and pulled him under. Soon Tommy Tipp was there no more.

As if he'd never been there at all.

You see why I have reason to be suspicious. It was awfully convenient that the water nymphs were there right then, ready and hungry for fresh meat. One could almost think that it was planned, that Pepper-Man had it all set up. One of the water girls carried Tommy's eyes as diamonds for a long time after. I would cringe every time I saw them twinkling at me, dangling from a string between her breasts. I suppose she thought them as pretty as I did, once upon a time. I don't know what happened to the rest of him, but his heart.

I do know what happened to his heart.

After Tommy was gone, Pepper-Man and I sat down by the brook, watching the water rush by.

'He was supposed to take me away,' I said. 'He was supposed to be my way out of that house, away from the white room and Mother.'

'I know.' Pepper-Man's arm was looped around my shoulders.

'What am I to do now?'

'Wait for a new one.'

'That can take time. I'm not most men's first choice, you know.'

'Then most men are fools,' snorted Pepper-Man.

'I still need one, though, unless I leave for school.'

'You would leave us behind, then.' It was not a question.

'Not willingly.' My mind was racing through the options left for me: I could ignore people's talk and move out on my own, but work in S— was scarce, and it would take a great amount of time and patience to build enough experience to gain a decent income. I had been hoping that Tommy would take care of the money. Although how I had envisioned he would do that, I don't know. In my lust-fueled haze I suppose I'd just figured it would work itself out. I had never thought to ask if I was even in his plans.

I learned many a harsh lesson that summer.

'There might be another way,' said Pepper-Man, 'if you are willing to try.'

'What way?' My eyes were still on the water.

'You could bring Tommy back.'

I turned my head and looked at him. His icy beauty was stark in the sunlight. Flecks of green played on his skin where the light filtered through the branches above us.

'We could make another Tommy,' he explained. 'He would not be quite the same, but he would serve you well for a while.'

'Different how?'

'He would *look* the same, which would be the most important thing if we are to fool his family and friends, but we would bind him to you, like a servant. He would never leave you and he would never touch another. We can keep as much of his personality as you like, but I would remove everything but his memories, and give him some new skills, too. Make him take proper care of you.'

'When can we do this?' I was already on my feet, eager to undo what I'd just done.

Pepper-Man chuckled. 'Not so fast, my sweet. The work is hard and can easily fail. I will not promise that we succeed, but I do think we should try. None of us wants to see you wither in that room.'

'What do you want in return?' I knew very well that no faerie favors came for free.

'Besides your happiness?' His toes were wriggling on the ground, nearly touching the water. 'We will discuss that if we succeed. One more thing,' he added after I'd nodded in agreement, eager to get it done with. Eager to get on. 'He will not last forever . . . Work like this is fickle. Sooner or later the seams will burst.'

I nodded again, barely hearing a word he said. I wanted to make a new Tommy – make a new boyfriend and move on with my life.

'To the mound, then?' I asked, assuming that was where this *work* would happen.

'To the mound,' Pepper-Man confirmed, coming up close behind me.

***

Pepper-Man certainly didn't lie when he said the work was hard and fickle, littered with mistakes and setbacks.

When we arrived at the mound, an old faerie woman I'd named Harriet met us at the opening, carrying milk and honey cakes for me. She chuckled quietly in a way that let me know the whole mound was already buzzing with the news of what had happened.

'You are a dangerous girl to love, Cassie.' Her nose was wriggling, whiskers shivering.

'I think it was the *lack* of love that did him in.' Gwen came up behind her. She wore an old-fashioned headscarf to hide her ears, but the golden eyes and the fur coating on her naked breasts still gave her away. She would never pass for human; I'm not sure if she ever wanted to.

'The water girls brought the prize.' Harriet hurried inside

after us with the tray. 'Big and fat it was.' She motioned to a wooden bowl placed on a chair before one of the many fireplaces. In it lay Tommy Tipp's heart. The faeries, about a dozen of them, tall and small, stood around it, looking at it. When we arrived in the circle they made room: it was *our* prize, after all.

I had imagined the heart to be damaged somehow; small and shriveled or black with rot. It wasn't. It was fresh and fine, deep red and glistening like a polished jewel. Mara came to stand beside me and hold my hand. She was a young girl then, about fourteen by human standards. She wore some green and brown cotton skirts I had given her; they swept the floors when she moved. Brown feathers adorned her unruly hair, and her pale skin was dusted with freckles.

'Not to worry,' she said, softly in my head. 'He was already a lost cause.'

I squeezed her hand gratefully. 'I didn't mean to do it.'

'Better now, that we can make you a new one, than twenty years from now when you have slaved for him and strived for him.'

'It *is* a gift, I suppose.' I was still looking at the heart. 'Not many girls can build their husbands from scratch.'

'Take away the bad, add the sweet.'

'We only want to help.' Harriet put down the tray.

One of the water girls had lingered in the mound. She sat pale-eyed and water-drenched on a table, drying her hair. 'Tasted like wine.' She licked her lips. 'But he was tart, too, and bitter at times.'

'Aren't they all,' said Harriet.

'Give us some room,' said Pepper-Man, and the three of us stepped closer to the bowl while the others stepped back. Mara lifted her hand as if to touch the heart, but I stopped her halfway there.

'Don't. I don't trust him anymore.'

'He is dead,' said Mara.

'For the time being,' Pepper-Man reminded her.

Harriet, Francis and Gwen brought bundles of twigs, heaped them onto the floor.

Francis sorted the twigs into piles by size. 'Let's make Cassie a husband,' he beamed and sat down cross-legged on the floor. We joined him there and, one by one, chose twigs from the piles and set to twisting and braiding.

The new Tommy was a sorry sight at first, hastily made as he was, but Pepper-Man said the heart had to be fresh, so we were working against the clock – the faerie clock, as it was, which sometimes moves faster than ours. Tommy Tipp's new body looked much like a scarecrow, twig fingers pointing left and right, one leg slightly longer than the other, but Pepper-Man said that it wasn't important, the important thing was the idea of the man, not the anatomical proportions. Mara stuffed his chest with leaves and flowers, Harriet poured honey on his pelvis, enhanced now with a large stick of oak. Pepper-Man blew sand into his empty skull, Francis gave him river stones for eyes, and Gwen gave him lips of down. Finally, I crowned him with a flower wreath; braided with the stems were long strands of my hair. I suppose it was so he would think of me only.

We had left an empty cavern in the chest and Pepper-Man lifted the heart from the bowl and carefully placed it in there. We sealed the cavern with more leaves, glossy and green, and Harriet poured more honey on top – to make him kind, I think.

Then we waited. And waited. There was no magic spell, no potion to devour. Just waiting. All eyes on the wicker man on the floor, the new Tommy-to-be. There were more faeries around us now; at least twenty, maybe more. All of them were watching our handiwork. I still sat cross-legged on the dirt floor, closer than anyone to the lifeless wicker man. My heart kept fluttering, looking for signs; a twitch, a breath – anything that told me he was coming to life.

'Maybe we should have used roots.' Harriet was standing before me, hands on her broad hips.

'We could have filled him with the dirt soaked in his own blood from the place he fell,' Gwen added.

'Maybe his heart is too weak,' said Pepper-Man. 'Maybe he was even less than I thought.'

I started to cry again then, had so dearly been hoping that this was the answer. Mara came to comfort me and pressed her soft cheek to mine.

'There will be a search now,' I said. 'Annie's mother may tell on me.'

'Who would miss him?' asked Pepper-Man. 'They will think he left, he was that kind of man.'

I certainly couldn't argue with that. 'Maybe, but how can I escape the white room now?'

'Let us give it some more time,' said Harriet.

And we waited. And waited. The stick-Tommy didn't rise. I dried my tears repeatedly, clutching Mara to my chest.

'There *is* another way,' said Pepper-Man. 'It is not easy, but it can be done.'

'What?' I asked. 'What can be done?'

'I can carry him for a while.' A gasp went through the

assembly, whether in awe or mock surprise, I don't know. 'I could infuse the body with life, if I ate his heart.'

I shook my head in confusion. 'It would be you, then?'

'Yes and no. I would remember Tommy as well. I could not stay in that wicker cage all the time, but enough to be your husband and rescue you from your mother's house.'

'But you would have to work,' I reminded him. 'Keep a garden and go to barbecue parties.' I just couldn't picture it: Pepper-Man joining the world.

'I have always been hungry for life, as well you know. This way we can truly be together, you and I – man and wife – for a time.'

'Would you really do that for me?' I felt strangely touched.

'But of course I would,' he grinned. 'Anything for you, my Cassandra. You know I will always protect you.'

And so it was that by the end of that long and awful day my lover's heart was once again removed from a chest and placed on a cracked china plate. Pepper-Man ate it raw, carving it with a silver knife. The rest of us gathered around him at the table, watching every mouthful traveling from plate to lips. He was a greedy one, my Pepper-Man; not a smidge remained on the plate when he was done.

When he was quite finished with the meal, Pepper-Man kissed me on the lips, leaving a residue of my lover's heart behind.

'Not to worry, my love. It will all be good, just you see.'

Francis and Harriet had worked on the wicker man while Pepper-Man ate, removing all the stuffing we had left inside and hollowing out the back so Pepper-Man could climb inside. He wore the wicker like armor; it capsuled him in like a sarcophagus.

We all gathered up again, forming a circle around Pepper-Man in the wicker cage – and finally something happened: skin and tissue started to form and knit a coat of skin over the stick skeleton. The wood itself swelled and turned to meat and bone. The river-stone eyes turned a glorious blue, and pupils bled forth from their depths. The oak stick turned soft and limp between his legs, the down became rosy lips. Under the wreath, golden hair sprouted forth, falling into glistening locks. His fingers flexed. His lips parted, showing off rows of white teeth.

Then he drew a breath.

The whole mound seemed to quiver around us by that first deep breath of air.

Faeries don't usually breathe, mind you. It had been a very long time since Pepper-Man did that last.

Then he moved.

One step.

Two steps.

Then he hugged me, and kissed me, and looked like Tommy, and felt like Tommy, but smelled distinctly like Pepper-Man.

'I told you it would work,' he said in Tommy's voice, even with Tommy's sly accent.

Mara came to hug us both, overjoyed by this turn of events. 'You can be together now. You can live on the surface like humans do.'

And yes, indeed, we could do just that: live on the surface like normal people, with mortgage and flowerbeds and nine-to-five jobs.

Until the spell broke.

***

110

And that's how it went when Pepper-Man became my husband, and why Tommy Tipp was not what you thought he was.

It lasted us a good twelve years, that spell, fueled by Tommy Tipp's heart. When it finally ended, though, as we all know – it was a complete disaster.

But on the surface, Tommy – or what people assumed was Tommy – wasn't much changed at all. Already on that first night, after we made him that body of twigs, leaves, and river stones, he would go back to Tommy's parents' house and climb into Tommy's bed, with no one suspecting anything at all.

'How does it feel to be truly alive again?' I asked, looking at my lover in ash and oak. We were standing outside my parents' house then; night chill had arrived with a breath of frost. Still he held me close, tight to his chest, which was empty and void of heartbeats.

'Like I could eat a mountain of beef, dance all night, down a barrel of beer.'

'Be careful, though, you're not used to this yet. Make sure no one finds out.'

'Oh, Cassandra,' he laughed, 'don't worry. I will make them all believe in me – in *us*, and the life we'll have.'

After he kissed me farewell that night, pressed his down-soft lips to mine, he whispered in my ear: 'It will be fine now, Cassie. It will all be fine, just you see.' He sounded like Tommy, the words were Tommy's, phrases that Pepper-Man never used. He had ingested Tommy's heart, after all, and tasted every emotion there. He remembered every day of Tommy's life worth remembering. The scent was not Tommy's, though – was strong and peppery, faerie sweet.

But life suited him well, it did. His cheeks were rosy red,

his eyes sparkled merrily. There was a spring in his steps when he walked, moved those wicker feet down the sidewalk.

'Are you sure you know the way?' I called after his leather-clad back.

'Not to worry, Cassandra, my sweet. My head works just fine – just you see.'

14

The new Tommy Tipp was a better Tommy Tipp. He got up in the mornings and walked the streets of S— with his few good references in hand, one of them from the workshop at the prison, and finally landed an apprentice position with Barnaby, the local locksmith.

The irony wasn't lost on people. That a former convict should mend their locks and secure their doors from intruders. Sense overruled their concern, though. There was no way a man would illegally enter a home where he'd just installed the locks himself. For this reason alone my husband became quite popular in his new profession. A good luck charm, if you will, a protection against malice.

To me it made perfect sense. Pepper-Man had always been good with his hands; those long, wiry fingers that could braid and twist branches into gifts. He was also fascinated with people's homes, the way that they lived, and this job let him see quite a few. He was fast and efficient. Barnaby loved the new Tommy.

And all his nights were spent with me.

***

'Maybe Tommy was tired of playing around,' Dr Martin said when I finally told him the truth. We were in the hospital, just before the trial. 'Maybe you hitting him like that in the woods made him realize that he hurt people? Maybe he wanted another life, and some bloodshed made him realize how far off the track he'd wavered? You could have done him a favor by pushing him onto that rock. Maybe you helped him get his priorities straight?'

'Tommy Tipp didn't feel anything at that point. He was dead and eaten by the water girls.'

'Don't you think that the anger you felt in that moment of betrayal might have made you *want* to see Tommy dead? That it felt safer for you after what you saw in your *love spot* to stuff your old friend Pepper-Man inside him? It made it easier to relate, didn't it, to a man that wasn't a man?'

'He wasn't a man. He was a faerie.'

Dr Martin chuckled then, without any malice, mind you. 'It's usually the other way around, you know. Usually, if we see something "alien" in our spouses, we get frightened, and sometimes, if we're a little confused, we call that stranger in our loved one's shell "the devil" or "a demon" or something along those lines . . . I have had other patients in my time who swore their husbands or wives turned into something else, some entity with evil intent. Hell, I think we all feel like that sometimes, when watching our partners change across the breakfast table, that something bad is afoot, destroying what we hold most dear . . . It is just people changing, though – falling out of love, perhaps. It is different for you, though, you *wanted* your Tommy replaced with a being. For you, that was the safer option. As a man among men, I can't entirely blame you.'

'I didn't have to want anything. Pepper-Man became Tommy because he wanted to – because I needed him to. Although I have been thinking lately that he might have planned that outcome all along. Maybe Pepper-Man *wanted* to be Tommy Tipp. Maybe that was his plan.'

'To experience humanity?'

'To experience humanity – again.'

'That doesn't sound much like the Pepper-Man of your childhood. The one who gave you such sleepless nights. Why do you think he changed?'

I didn't answer the question truthfully, as I knew Dr Martin would not understand. I don't think Pepper-Man changed to suit my needs, as he himself would have me believe. I think he changed because *I* changed. That is the curse of the faeries, you see, they are ever changing, evolving, adapting – struggling to hold on to a core of self. They are like air, in a way, or water: they react to shifts in temperature and environment, and, of course, to what they eat.

The key is in the diet. Always.

He changed because he'd fed from me for so long and adopted traits of humanity through his nourishment. Through me, he learned to be a man again, but let me make one thing clear: Pepper-Man is ever self-serving, just like any other faerie. My well-being is his well-being; my path is his path – he needs me more than I need him. Back then, when he was Tommy, I was still the source of the experience he craved as well as his source of life.

Was there ever romance between us? Sure. But it was always so much more than that. The love was just a game – the *hunger* was always what counted. And Pepper-Man liked living through me; grew strong and fat and very lucid – vivid – when he fed from me. I think my blood resonated more deeply with his almost forgotten humanity than, say, the sap of a birch tree or the heart blood of a fox.

I think he was a very dangerous man when he was alive, way back in time. He must have had a honeyed tongue and persuasion must have been his gift. I picture him a merchant prince, counting golden coins. There's no point in asking, he doesn't remember a thing. But it's still there, the template, the basic blueprint of who he once was. Ruthless and cunning, that's my Pepper-Man, no matter his pleasing exterior.

Maybe I adapted too, and learned to live *with* the monster instead of struggling against it. If I did, it happened such a long time ago, I cannot recall how that felt, being afraid of Pepper-Man. He was ugly at first, for sure, and I always worried about what he would do, but then – he was always there beside me, a steady companion who knew me more intimately than anyone else, and my only champion for so long. There was much comfort in that. He did what Mother could not and gave me a sense of self-worth. To him I was precious – even if only as his source of existence.

You can't get more important than that, after all.

These latter years he has changed again, paling to a dusty gray.

I think that means I might be changing too, slowly shedding my colors with age. I wonder what I will look like at the end. When I walk out the door to this house for the very last time.

Will I even recognize myself in the mirror?

***

After he became Pepper-Man, drinking and gambling was no longer Tommy's habit. That first winter of his new life, before we got married, he left his human vices behind, and instead we would go for long walks through the streets of S— and have ice cream by the sea. He took me to the movies and bought me pastries and roses.

The women Tommy Tipp used to have relations with

observed this new development with suspicion and jealousy. Soon there was a rumor that I had fallen pregnant, and that Tommy stood by me because it was 'the right thing to do', and he was a good man, really. When time went on and no baby was in sight, they said I'd either tricked him or miscarried.

The rumors made Mother uncomfortable.

'He should make a decent woman out of you,' she said. 'No need to feed the gossip mill. God knows it would be better for all of us if you left this house for good.'

She didn't care at all that Tommy Tipp had so recently been considered 'bad news'. I think any man would have done for her, as long as someone pulled me out of her hair. I think that if she could, she would have rather just forgotten I existed.

After seven months as Tommy the locksmith, Pepper-Man did as Mother wished, and married me the first day of May. The wedding took place at the S— town hall. Tommy Tipp's mother and aunts donned dresses in powder blue and salmon pink, pulled straw hats down their ears, and came to throw rice as we exited the stairs. His parents hosted a barbecue after the short ceremony; there was beer and food and we popped champagne. My dress was blue silk; bought at a second-hand store. The diamond on my finger was new, bought with locksmith money. My parents were absent, though they sent flowers and a card. Olivia and Ferdinand, the latter freshly dropped out of college, made an appearance late at the barbecue. My sister wore a champagne-colored dress that made her look old and matronly. Ferdinand wore a wrinkled shirt and a tie with tiny elephants on it. He had a beer. Olivia nibbled on a chicken leg.

'You didn't want them to come, right?' Ferdinand asked,

when the clock had struck midnight. Olivia had long since gone home and one beer for my brother had – with surprising ease – become many more.

'Mother and Father? No – of course not.'

'Good. I would hate for them to not show, if you really had wanted them to.'

'Did they say anything, at home? About why they didn't?'

'She said it wasn't "their kind of celebration", the barbecue . . . You know Mother can be a bit of a snob. I am happy for you, though. Olivia too – we both are.'

'Tell Mother I said thanks for the flowers. Tell them I thought it was thoughtful and sweet.'

See? I was already learning to pretend. Say the right things to appease the beasts.

With a few years, I would master it fully, and so would Pepper-Man-in-Tommy. We were strangers in disguise, living there among them.

No one ever suspected a thing.

***

After all the dirty plates were gathered and carried inside, every empty beer can located among the trees and shrubbery in the Tipp family's garden, Pepper-Man-in-Tommy and I went into the woods, where we married again at the mound.

Pepper-Man and I had no need of rites of blood, to cut and mingle our life-streams, we had already done so long ago. Neither would we jump the broom, knowing there would be no more fruits. We just celebrated ourselves, and looked forward to our life together – and my freedom from the white room. We lifted our cups to Tommy Tipp, to his heart, that hard and stringy organ that had brought us to this bliss.

Pepper-Man left his Tommy-shell, dressed up in red, and

danced with me, fast and wild. The piper and the drummer whipped up a shrilling reel, a feisty waltz, and a tango so dangerous it cut our legs with its razor-sharp edges. Mara danced too, skirts a haze, changing partners faster than the music could follow. The honey cakes were plentiful; stacked with red apples far out of season and sugared nuts and violets. Sweet wine ran from barrels down into bottomless cups. My blue silk dress ripped, my left heel broke. The diamond on my finger sparkled. Mara pressed a kiss to my lips, her skin was warm and flushed from dancing. She placed a wedding crown on my brow, made from wild roses, hawthorn, moths, and silver bells.

'A faerie bride,' she whispered. 'That is what my mother is.'

'A faerie child,' I whispered back. 'That is what my daughter is.'

***

I guess that through all this you have started to wonder about Mara. Who is this person so dear to me, yet absent from your mother's memories, this woman who draws me to the mound and calls me Mother? The young girl I have been fighting with – and warning you about, though perhaps not strongly enough?

I'll tell you about Mara, and how she came to be.

***

My little girl came about when I was fourteen. She was an accident – the result of my brief stint as a fertile woman.

I was wholly unprepared for puberty in that way. Didn't expect to wake up on sticky sheets, see Pepper-Man trail the blood with his fingers and stare at it, as if mesmerized. I had some idea of how these things worked, of course, I was no fool and I had read books, of course, but I hadn't expected it to be quite as grisly.

'The blood means you are ripe for plucking.' Pepper-Man stretched out behind me, placing a hand on my aching belly, on the faint swell that had appeared overnight. 'You can have children of your own now, make life in that tiny cauldron of yours.'

'What if I bleed out.' I pressed my face hard into the pillow; my voice was muffled by the down.

Pepper-Man chuckled behind me. 'You will not, women have bled always. It is the curse of your kind to sometimes bleed. Occasionally it will stop, and then it will begin again. There is no escaping the blood now, not before you are all worn out.'

'But it hurts.' I curled around my aching belly like a fetus.

'Who said it would be painless to carry such a gift? The blood is the price for life, it has always been so.' He swept one of his long fingers across the bloody sheets, and lifted the index to his lips to taste.

'Make it stop,' I demanded. 'I know you can do that.'

'Why, not even I can turn back the course of time. You are ripe when you are ripe, and your blood will be even fatter for it. Taste better.'

I remember something shattering in me at that moment; breaking into pieces like a kaleidoscope.

For a brief moment, I saw it all, felt it all: how he stole from me. How he reveled in my blood – my pain – and lived on it, and for the very first time, it bothered me.

'I give *you* life.' I meant it to be an accusation.

He chuckled beside me, fingers back on my belly, resting. 'That you do, and what a fine source of life you are.'

'You never asked me if it was all right.'

'It is a natural thing to feed. You never asked your Sunday roast if it cared to be your meal.'

'I thought you loved me,' said I.

'I do! I do! How can one not love blood as rich as yours? You have made me who I am, sustained my very being, and for that I will be forever at your service.'

'For a price.'

'There is always a price. Anything worth having has a price.'

'What is *my* price tag, then?' I asked. 'What do I get in return for what I give you?'

'I am your servant, bound by blood and shadow. Isn't that enough?'

And it was, because it had to be. Without Pepper-Man I was nothing, just a sad and angry girl. Without him, all I had was the shrinking white room and a family that loathed me. No magic, then, no crowns of twigs – no midnight flights in the otherworld and dancing until dawn. No mound and no woods, just me, all alone. No one would love and take care of me then.

So I had bled, every month or so, for a year. Those intervals were days of aching, of hunger and fatigue, raging and tears. Mother bought me pads, but said little on the subject. Her furious attitude had turned into a quiet sort of resentment. She would rather not see the woman I became, just as she never wanted to see the child I was before. Her greatest failing, I think, was to always see me for what I was *not*, never for what I was.

***

Motherhood done right is not a thing of beauty. The bonds that bind run deep, are shackles of love forged deep under your skin. Root and thorn; blood and bone; pain and suffering . . . It's an instinctual love that has nothing to do with reason and you can never ask your children for something in return.

Maybe there was something wrong with Mother, who didn't feel that way about me. Maybe she, too, was broken from the start?

Dr Martin thought so, back then, and later on. Maybe she was afraid, he reasoned, her rules were nothing but desperate ways of keeping her own demons at bay. She let other demons into my bed, though, and pretended not to see.

I will never forgive her for that.

She made me love my Pepper-Man, because there was no one else to love. Made me rely on him always, because there was no one else to trust.

What kind of mother *does* that?

***

My fourteenth birthday came and went, and suddenly I bled no more. The well was dry, I thought at first. There would be no more bleeding, I had withered before my time.

Then I got stomachaches and threw up before breakfast.

'You carry a child.' Pepper-Man stood beside the porcelain bowl, looking at me as I heaved above the toilet.

'I don't think so,' I croaked and fished a towel from the rack to dry residue from my lips and beads of moisture from my brow.

'I know these things.' Pepper-Man's voice was calm as snow. 'You carry a child within you.'

I would like to say that my world shattered at that point, that I was struck by lightning and lamented my cruel fate for days on end, but I didn't. I was still a girl, you see, still stuck in that place in between worlds, that crystalline haze of not-quite-there. Reality didn't have sharp enough edges, daylight wasn't harsh enough to penetrate to where I was. So at first, I did nothing but throw up and wipe my lips, let Pepper-Man soothe me with gifts of leaves and thorny branches. Then my body started to change: a dark trail appeared across my abdomen, from my navel and down to my sex. My small breasts ached and the nipples swelled. I put my hand on my belly and thought I could feel life pulsating through my skin, just below my fingertips. It felt mysterious and alien, yet magical and sweet. The connection to the embryo was instantaneous and strong. It was mine. I felt that.

The child was mine.

15

This is where things get ugly, I'm afraid. No good thing – no spell – ever lasted.

I woke up one night, ice cold and sweating. My sheets were sticky again, and this time it was a lot. I screamed when I saw it, or wanted to scream, but it came out just a sad and wailing sound. All that blood pouring out of me; my hopes, my love, just slipping away between my thighs. I writhed on the mattress, on that slick pool of red.

'Pepper-Man!' I cried out. 'Pepper-Man!'

'I am here,' he said calmly. He was in the white wicker chair by the window, thin curtains billowing in and obscuring his pale form. His voice was somber, his face chiseled in the semi-darkness.

'What is this?' I asked him. 'Why is this happening?'

'It is a faerie child you carry. It was never meant to walk this earth.'

'But why?' I sat up shivering; knelt on the mattress with the sheets a twist around my feet, flecked with stains of blood.

'It cannot live like you do, it belongs to the mound, like me. That is the curse of faerie.'

'No.' My voice was just a whisper. 'My child can't die. I won't let it.' I doubled over in pain again, pressed my face against the pillow while a fresh wave of nauseating pain coursed through my body.

Pepper-Man rose from the chair then, reached out a hand. 'Then come with me now, come to the mound. Maybe there is still a chance! Maybe we can save the child!'

Silently I took his fingers. I tried to stand up, but I couldn't, so he gathered me in his arms and we set off; jumped out through the window and down on the chilly lawn, went into the woods, between the silent trees.

My consciousness was slipping then; the sky above became a blur. The dark blue night and the tall, black treetops bled together, became wings before my vision. My nightgown was soaked through; Pepper-Man's hands were slick. My child was leaving me, drop by shiny drop.

'You knew it all along,' I accused Pepper-Man in a faint voice.

'Yes.'

'But I have heard of others, half-faerie, half-man . . .'

'Those are just in your books.'

'I don't believe you,' I argued weakly, only because I didn't *want* to believe.

'Those few who live to birth are weak and sickly. We leave them in cradles and take healthy children back in their stead, to soothe the mothers, mostly. Our kinds were never meant to breed, my Cassandra. We are like day and night, light and darkness, life and death.'

'A twilight child.'

'Just that.' I could hear that he was smiling.

'But it can live in the mound?'

'Maybe it can, if we arrive there in time.'

'You should have told me.'

Pepper-Man didn't reply to that.

In the mound they laid me on a mattress filled with hay and herbs. Harriet brought me a draught to drink. Gwen stripped me of my clothes, smoothed the wet tendrils of my hair and wiped perspiration from my brow. They spread my legs wide and looked at the damage.

'Faerie births are never easy.' Harriet shook her head.

'Oh, she comes through just fine.' Gwen was looking at the bloody mess.

'Her?' I asked.

'It is a girl.' Gwen's eyes were shimmering gold.

They had cleared the space before one of the fireplaces, the very same spot where we would make Tommy Tipp some years later. There was a fire blazing, water and herbal concoctions boiling in copper pots. The air in there was dense and warm, scented of blood and greenery, faintly of decay.

The other faeries had withdrawn to the other side of the room or left the mound altogether. I was grateful. It felt like a courtesy, them doing this for me, giving me some space in my desperate hour of need.

Pepper-Man was there, though, quiet sentinel, feeding the flames with oak, ash, and thorn, aiming for a smooth passage.

'If she pulls through, she must stay here with us.' Harriet caught my gaze with hers, warning me, perhaps. 'She can never live out there with you. She would wither then, be gone for good. She was never meant to live.'

I nodded silently, gulped down what I could from the wooden cup presented to me. It tasted harsh and bitter. Tasted like defeat. Any life would do, though. Any life for my girl.

'Now you must sleep,' Harriet said, and when the herbal

brew laced my system, I did. Even through the pain, through the waves that ripped me apart, I slept.

Then, when I woke up again, my life had changed forever.

***

She was such a tiny thing at first, my Mara, lying there on an oak leaf. We fed her my milk from a rosy red petal and covered her body in soft downs. Pepper-Man made her a cradle from twigs, and the spiders spun her a dress of silk. Every day after school I walked to the mound to take care of my little daughter. I let Harriet take my milk and my blood to feed her when I was gone. She grew fast, though: within a month, she was the size of a newborn child. Within the year, she looked like a girl of five; brown of hair, blue of eyes, beautiful in every way. She stopped aging when she reached adulthood, has been a young woman now for years. Radiant and healthy, always.

Isn't that what all parents wish for their children? That they will grow up and be strong?

There would be no other children, though. Faerie births are hard, and I was never quite the same again after. The medical exam Dr Martin had me do before the trial only confirmed that fact: my womb is broken – torn and poorly mended.

The mound itself is a womb for the dead, spewing out twisted life, and that is where my daughter lives, safe and protected, always.

***

There is another version of this story, but I am not sure of its origins.

It could have been Dr Martin, coaxing me and twisting my mind. He did that sometimes, asked and asked until I gave in and made up other stories, just to make him stop.

In that story, I am sitting at the table with my family. It's another Sunday dinner; roast or ham or something glistening at the centre of the table. Olivia is sullen for some reason. Her pouty lower lip quivers as she chews through the meat. Her long lashes fan out on her creamy skin, her gaze is glued to the plate.

Ferdinand, home for the weekend, is just at the onset of puberty himself. He is a pale shadow by the table, playing with the brussels sprouts on his plate with the fork; rolling the green balls back and forth between the heaps of meat and the sickly white potatoes. No gravy for Ferdinand, he likes things neat.

Mother at her end is folding and refolding the napkin in her hands. Her coral-red fingernails are smoothing the soft paper repeatedly. She isn't eating, she is chewing her lips. All her lipstick is gone and I can see her swallow and swallow. Her eyes look wrong, like shattered crystals; something is broken in there. I think she might have been crying – or if she hasn't already, that she is about to very soon. This is a rare thing, it barely happens.

Father is somber. He's serving himself more potatoes, pours more gravy on top. He doesn't look at us. Doesn't look at Mother. He is looking at his food, and his lips stretch, and he eats. Mother looks at him, though, expression somewhere between pleading and fury. Occasionally she looks at me and her face goes blank. She is ice and smooth, like white stone.

'I'm doing better in school this term.' Ferdinand's voice is very quiet.

'Good,' says Mother. 'That is good.'

Father chews. Olivia sulks. Ferdinand falls back into silence.

'Cassie, how are you these days?' Mother's voice has a shrill edge to it.

'Fine,' I say, or rather whisper. Truth is I am not fine. I am sick a lot, I throw up. I have a baby in my belly.

'No more trouble at school, I hope?'

It hasn't really been more trouble than usual – those days I kept the snide girls and bullies at bay by being scary, by telling stories about Pepper-Man. I would glare and scowl and say he had taught me to perform a curse: *How to make beauty fade.* They would snigger and roll their eyes, but stay away; no one wants to be ugly. The teachers were always complaining about my lack of effort, about my poor attention span. Even the ones who appreciated my 'considerable imagination' had given up on me, but I didn't grieve the loss. I had too many things going on, too many things to think about.

None of this is new, though, which is why I get suspicious when Mother asks.

'Have you gotten any new friends?' She folds the napkin, unfolds the napkin.

'No.' I am surprised by the question. She really ought to know better than that.

'No?' She repeats it as a question, biting into her lip. 'No . . . boys?'

'No,' I blurt out, eyes widening – the idea is silly.

Mother gives me a shivering smile, goes back to mock eating, pushing pieces of meat onto her fork with the knife, but never lifting it to her lips. 'I think you have looked so pale recently. Are you eating well? Not developing some affliction, are you?'

'No.' It's starting to get uncomfortable now, and I know where this is headed. She has figured it out, what is going on, or at least developed a strong suspicion.

'Well.' Mother's fork is still hovering in the air. 'You would tell me, wouldn't you? If something was wrong?' She says that last part with a hard edge, gaze darting across the table, toward Father.

'Of course.' I can feel my cheeks flush. I had never planned on telling, I think. I had somehow believed that the baby was mine and mine alone, that it was just another secret to keep. Now I saw that I had been wrong. This particular secret spilled out, was just as real to others as it was to me. The realization rattled me. Now it was I who swallowed hard and fought to chew through the meat.

'Cassie is getting fat,' said Olivia.

'No,' said my mother, voice stern, gaze mended. 'She's not.'

***

In the next part of this story, I am sitting in the back seat of the family car. It is a large brown one with a spacious trunk, but I couldn't tell you the brand. Father's hands are on the wheel, his eyes are peering back at me from the rear-view mirror. In the passenger seat beside him is Mother, wearing a navy-blue coat of wool. She has a pocket mirror in her hand, is freshening up her lipstick. I can see her reflection from where I'm sitting. Her eyes look tired, and small cakes of pale powder are haphazardly strewn around her face. I think she's looking old. Older than before. Only her curls are as they have always been; very yellow, very hard.

'Don't drive so fast,' she tells Father. 'We'll get there soon enough.' She doesn't sound very enthusiastic about the prospect. 'Although I guess you are eager to have it dealt with.' Her voice is pure venom, laced with loathing.

Father says nothing, he just drives on through the barren landscape in the early hours of dawn. The first hint of winter has come, coating the fields in a thin crust of ice. It'll melt again in a matter of hours, but the skeletal fingers of frost have definitely been there, warning of the season to come.

I'm in pain.

'How are you doing back there?' Mother half turns in her seat to look at me. 'I'm sure you are eager to get there as well?' Her voice is not as toxic as before, but it holds no warmth either. Again, she has that wary expression when she looks at me, as if I am a potential danger, as if I might bite. As if I'm something she can't handle and she knows it. There is no blame in there, but no compassion either.

I don't say anything. I feel sick.

'You should have told us earlier.' Mother's lips are pursed when she looks into the mirror. 'It gets harder the longer you wait.'

'How do *you* know?' I'm not trying to hide my resentment.

Mother doesn't answer my question. 'You don't have to tell Dr Martin about this,' she says instead.

'Why?'

'He would only make a fuss.'

'Why?'

'Because that's what doctors do.'

'You were the one who wanted me to see him.'

'I know,' she sighs, closes the mirror and puts it back in her purse; her gaze drifts out the window. 'We don't have to tell everyone everything,' she says. 'Some things ought to stay in the family.' Father grunts his approval by her side. She turns to him, snaps: 'You don't get to have a say in this.' Back to me: 'You just say it was a boy if they ask you when we get there.'

'What boy?' I feel utterly miserable. Angry, too.

Mother shrugs. 'A boy from school. They won't ask for names.'

We drive on.

Halfway there, we have to stop so I can throw up. I'm standing by the roadside, retching, holding my hair away from my face. I am wearing an oversized shirt to hide my 'condition', one of Father's old work shirts, I think. It smells like copper and peppery cologne.

Mother is leaning against the car, looking in the opposite direction. Her sunglasses have huge frames – making her look like she has insect eyes. Father is standing on the other side of the car; in the middle of the road, staring into the horizon. He doesn't look at me.

***

The clinic was as one expects such places to be: sterile, cold, white and silver, softened by a touch of turquoise. No one asked me about the boy. The nurses were kind but impersonal and everyone spoke in hushed voices, as if they – like Mother – just wanted to get it over with.

I remember the cold surface of the operating table, remember the hard mattress in my lonely recovery, the smell of fabric softener from the bedsheets. A woman cried and spoke in Spanish on the other side of the pink curtain separating our beds. A faint scent of roses lingered in the air.

No roses for me, though, but on our way back I was given a box of caramel cupcakes. Father bought them for me in a store nearby the hospital. I didn't eat them, I was too sick and still in pain. I dozed the whole way home. When we got there, I stuffed the cupcakes under the bed, then I lay back on the bedspread and cried.

Pepper-Man wasn't there.

I was alone.

***

As I said before, I don't know where this second story comes from, but Dr Martin wrote about it in *Away with the Fairies: A Study in Trauma-Induced Psychosis*. It's one of the things that made your mother so angry with me, I suppose.

They said it never happened, Mother and Olivia, but Dr Martin certainly thought it had. He had them examine me before the trial, and felt the results proved him right. Something had indeed happened to me; the doctor who examined me was very clear on that. Dr Martin could never track down the clinic, though. Neither he nor my lawyer could find anyone who would have remembered me. None of this existed in any file.

'Your parents are well connected,' Dr Martin said. We were talking in 'our' room at the hospital, during my trial. 'I am sure they found a way to cover their tracks.'

'Why does it matter?'

'It could mean a lot to the jury.'

'Why?' I asked, though even I realized the importance.

'A broken and traumatized woman is no murderer, not in any common sense. You shouldn't go to prison, Cassie, you should stay here at the hospital.'

'I don't know if I remember it right,' I argued. 'And my daughter isn't even dead. She is living in the woods, in the mound, still.'

'Exactly.' Dr Martin smiled a tired smile. 'Which only proves my point. Have you ever thought about *why* there are two stories about what happened in there?' He touched my forehead gently across the table.

I shrugged. I knew what was true, of course. I knew that my Mara was safe and sound, but the other story was still there, made up or not, and Dr Martin so dearly wanted to believe it. 'Can't both stories be true?' I asked. 'Why is it that only because one thing is true, the other thing is not? Why do we always have to decide?'

He chuckled then. 'You really are something, Cassie . . . Don't you think we need a foundation of truth to measure what's false?'

'Like science?'

'Just that.'

I didn't know what to say at first. How could I describe what I felt inside, that 'truth' to me was like mercury, always changing, moving – didn't matter? I could easily hold two strings of truth in my mind and feel them both to be real without getting all confused about it. Now I realize that's not how most people feel, but then I was far more oblivious.

Truth is such a fickle thing, isn't it? Subjective and shifting like a living being.

Pepper-Man or no Pepper-Man – that's just two sides of the same coin. Two sides of the same Cassie-coin. It all depends on which side you look at.

I could see them both.

***

I could stop here. I would like to stop here. I am old now and tired. I'm thinking I should stop typing now and let the past be. But then you would still have questions. Questions about the body in the woods, questions about what happened later – those other deaths that occurred . . . I guess I owe you some answers about that. The 'family tragedy'. The violent end. *Somebody* ought to know what really happened.

And so I keep writing – and you two keep reading.

16

We had lived together for twelve years, Mr and Mrs Tommy Tipp, in that small brown house on the outskirts of S—. We had even bought a lawnmower from Father's firm, which Pepper-Man-in-Tommy pushed around in the garden every Sunday, toweling off perspiration with crumpled-up T-shirts and drinking cold beers on his breaks. I would watch him through the windows sometimes, making roast and salads in the kitchen, using freshly picked vegetables from our own patch. I was quite the housewife, back then. When I felt particularly inspired, I even made raspberry and blackcurrant spreads, canned fruits and mixed herbal teas.

I grew sated in those years. My hips rounded and my braid fell long and thick down my back, looking all lustrous and healthy – Pepper-Man loved it, played with it for hours. Those were my years of milk and gravy.

Pepper-Man-in-Tommy was the perfect husband; I never had to worry that he would stray or leave me. The two of us were so strongly entwined, so mingled and as one, separation seemed impossible. Still does.

I remember that first day at our new home, when we carried the things from the white room inside; the cardboard boxes of books I had long since outgrown, the wicker chair, the fairytale pictures – how out of place it all seemed on the vast, wooden floor of our new living room. I placed it all in the attic, and the attic is where it still is. You can have a look for yourself; I had it all moved when I came here. The white room is neatly boxed up above your heads – all those bitter nights.

I had decided I wanted to be like the rest. Be like those other – *good* – women. It was easier that way, you see. Being different is hard and takes a toll. The rest of society is always pushing, herding us strays toward what it deems natural and decent and safe. Easier then to give in, I figured, pretend to be like everybody else. Even with a dreary reputation like mine, it was still doable, I believed, if I built those walls strong enough and painted the backdrop of my life in loud and cheery colors. Maybe if I kept my head down and dazzled all of S— with my pretty illusions, they would all think me happy and well adjusted, and I could at last get an ounce of peace.

Time to create. Time to explore. Time to walk between the worlds.

I didn't write professionally yet, that came later, after the trial. I dabbled in it, though, and painted and worked on some other arts as well.

My masterpiece from that time was doubtlessly my life. In that respect, I was no different from other young women. Every choice I made – from picking out a sofa, to choosing a profession for my man – was a measured move, a careful staging. Those four walls, that husband and that car, everything was calculated and carefully thought through. It had to appear solid and true to the world, you see. Every young wife can relate to that. If you can make your life a piece that fits neatly in the puzzle, you are all set and bound for that bland brand of happiness that people think they crave. Just look at your mother, Olivia did it too – she always excelled at it. Unlike many other girls, however, I didn't build my doll's house or raise those pretty screens to hide some petty mundane blemishes – alcohol problems, a lack of love, or a crushing, bottomless debt.

I was protecting rather than hiding.

Protecting my other life; the one that brought me endless joy; steeping my faerie tea, running through the woods, spending days on end with Mara in the mound.

So, you see, no matter what your mother thought at the time, or what she has told you, that I was 'well for a while', that things were peachy back then, she was wrong.

She didn't know me at all.

***

Dr Martin came to visit sometimes, drank iced tea in the garden. I remember him complimenting me on my 'radiant health' and admiring my 'harmonious lifestyle'.

'So close to nature,' he would say, glancing at the surrounding woods with a hint of suspicion.

The closeness to the woods was important, of course, when we chose where we would live. Easy access to the mound and Mara was number one on my list. Otherwise, we decided to keep a faerie-free environment, nothing unusual for our neighbors to see; no overgrown lawn or crowns of twigs, no faerie tea jars on display.

On the surface, everything was clean and untangled, fitting right in with the world around us. In our bedroom, however, or where no one cared to look, in closets and drawers, the nooks and crannies, nature burst forth: green leaves sprouted and moss lined the walls. Spider sisters spun sheets of silk around our bed, toadstools grew in our basement, and in the garden lived a tribe of frogs. That's what it's like being married to a faerie; the woods are never far off. Sometimes you have to pluck rowan leaves and hawthorn berries out of your laundry; throw out gallons of curdled milk; nap the fresh sprouts of buttercups or daisies from the sink. There is always debris; leaves and pieces of bark and twigs. Seeds and pollen. Dead things on the windowsills.

Visitors never saw that, though. They only saw our clean and spacious rooms; the cozy blue couch, the white tiles in the bathroom, the dining room set of oak with eight chairs. Barnaby's locksmith and hardware business was a good trade for a young husband like mine; the money allowed me to stay at home with my typewriter and my tea. I didn't write to sell yet, mind you, it was only for me and my Pepper-Man to see. My stories back then were just drafts of what was to come; rough coal sketches to the oil paintings I would make later, filling in the blanks with color and emotions. I never wrote about faeries, though. Never wrote about strange creatures living all around us, in the rustle you hear behind you on the street or the draft of icy wind that passes through your living room. No, instead I wrote about sinful seductions, indulgent romance and piña coladas, office intrigues and family dramas. That's what I found in the faerie tea: stories about normal people, about lives I'd never live.

That was exotic to me, you see, human lives without faerie implications. Was exotic to *them* as well, human lives untainted by death and rebirth – so that's what's captured in those jars: stories rife with flavors, scents, feelings, and trivial worries.

Dr Martin tried a cup once, after we'd discussed them at length. He'd suggested that the faerie tea was nothing but alcohol, and that the leaves and the flowers, the stones and the pieces of bark in the jars, were nothing but various forms of pills. Clearly he thought I was drinking my days away, dissolving pills in vodka and gin. I was horribly offended, of course, and sought to prove him wrong.

It was a lush autumn afternoon, just after my trial.

He was sitting on the porch at the brown house where I had returned to live after my acquittal.

'Tastes like grass and water.' He smacked his lips. 'What did you say it was? An acorn and a leaf?'

I nodded.

'Now what then? I go home and dream?'

'No. You just go about your day. The story will come to you; unfold like a flower, subtly – deep inside.'

He claimed it didn't work, but of course it did. It became *Away with the Fairies: A Study in Trauma-Induced Psychosis.* I guess it worked a little different on him, being unused to the faerie side of things.

***

If I have one regret from our time at the brown house, it's that we didn't allow Mara to come inside. Thinking back, it seems harsh, though she never seemed to mind, she was as happy as before whenever I came to visit. This house is different, though, even closer to the mound so she can come and go as she pleases – that is why I bought it in the first place. It was run down and neglected when I got it for nothing, the strip of road was overgrown. But I saw potential here. Saw the lilac beauty it could be.

I *had* to move, you see. When that wave of curious horror following the trial and the uproar around Dr Martin's book had subsided, people didn't fear me as much anymore. The village youth started to drive by in their cars, throwing eggs and other nastiness at the walls of our little brown house. I found letters reciting Bible verses on my porch and a dead rat in my mailbox.

Out here, there's no way to come and go unseen.

Dr Martin was horrified at the prospect of me moving so far into the woods all alone. He said it wasn't safe, but I knew it would be. I would move further into faerie land, so that their power would be stronger – would keep me safe, as it always had. And time has proven me right, hasn't it? There's been no more verses on my porch or dripping foodstuffs. I am merely an eccentric old lady now, 'that writer out in the woods', solitary in her secluded home, doing whatever eccentrics do.

People have almost forgotten about the trial, and about those other deaths too. That's what people do: they forget and they move on.

Not your mother, though.

Olivia will never forget.

If you are still with me, we should move on too.

17

The night Tommy Tipp died in the eyes of the world, we had known for some time that something wasn't right. I guess it was akin to cancer for other people, that slow onset of a disease you know can only end in misery. Of course, Pepper-Man-in-Tommy's disease played out a little differently.

At first, it was just small things: a twig peeking out of the skin on his thigh, a root coming loose by his ear lobe, then the honeyed oak stick stopped working and his hips became all skewered. His colleagues at Barnaby's thought it might be gout, and wanted him to go see a doctor. He never did, of course, what was the use in that? We knew very well that the body was falling apart, that the last few drops of Tommy Tipp's heart blood were slowly burning to an end. It didn't matter much to us, really, Pepper-Man had another body he could use, but we still despaired – it was our life together as man and wife that was coming to an end.

I pleaded with Pepper-Man to find a solution: 'What if you eat another heart, and we built a new body from scratch?'

'I wouldn't look like Tommy then.'

'Maybe we can say that Tommy left me for someone else and then I found myself another husband?'

'Would you really go through it all again, Cassandra? Build a new life with a different decoy?'

'Wouldn't you?' I asked.

'Not particularly.'

Pepper-Man was not wearing Tommy's body right then, it had grown uncomfortable and was hard to move around. He was sitting by the kitchen table cleaning his teeth with a straw. The carcass of a bird lay before him on a plate, all void of meat. He'd developed a taste for seasoned flesh as Tommy.

'I have tired of this game. It has been interesting, being Tommy Tipp, but I do miss my freedom. It is hard being a slave to the mortal clock.'

'You did it for me, though, I will never forget that.' I sat down before him, cradling a cup of faerie tea.

'It is just a matter of days now before the body is all spent. We should rid ourselves of it before you have to wheel it around in a chair.'

'But *how* do we get rid of it?'

'We take it down in the basement and dissemble it with the cleaver.'

'Easy as that, huh?'

'Yes, my Cassandra, just like that.'

'But what do we tell people? This is poorly thought through. They will ask where he is, you know. Barnaby will—'

'You could say that he left you, or that he had an unfortunate accident.'

'I don't want people to think that he left me.'

'We could put him under the car and say he was doing some tinkering, then something came loose and crushed his skull. Maybe the car began to roll—'

'Maybe he was painting the east wall.' I was suddenly inspired. 'It's been peeling for some time now, and then he fell down the ladder.'

'A very clever idea; such falls may cause a lot of damage.'

'Won't he be just twigs and leaves when he hits the ground?'

'The glamour will still hold for some time, long enough for people to be convinced he is dead.'

That settled, we went about our day. The next morning Pepper-Man was back in Tommy's body, showing up at work at exactly 8 a.m.

Things didn't go so smoothly later.

That same night, as Pepper-Man attempted to exit Tommy's body for his evening revels, the whole thing simply fell apart. Limbs and intestines tumbled to the floor, eyeballs rolled across the polished oak. His skin was like an empty sack, gaping open and stained with reeking fluids.

It was a disaster.

'Oh no,' I said, wringing my hands. 'What do we do now? *No one* will believe he fell off a ladder into all those pieces.'

Pepper-Man was leaning against the wall, arms crossed over his chest, taking in the mess. 'I cannot wear it again, that much is certain.'

'But what do we do? I can't let anyone see him – *it* – like this.'

'We could always carry the debris down in the basement. It will soon return to what it was before: twigs and stones and downs.'

'How long will it take, before it turns back?'

He shrugged. 'That depends.' Of course it did, it always did with Faerie.

'I think that it would smell, don't you?' I looked at the torn pieces of flesh. 'If we left it in the basement, it would smell before it turned back.'

'Outside, then, in the woods.'

'Someone might find it and mistake it for the real thing.'

'It might return to what it was faster out there. It was borrowed from the woods, after all, maybe the woods would welcome it back.'

'What do I say, then, that my husband left me?'

'That would certainly be the easiest.'

'Well.' I considered it. 'He *is* Tommy Tipp.'

'Tommy Tipp would certainly do that,' and Pepper-Man ought to know, having *been* Tommy Tipp for the last twelve years.

'Well, then,' I sighed. 'I guess I am abandoned.'

'Oh, sweet Cassandra,' Pepper-Man said with a smile. 'You know you will always have me.'

And so we transported the sad remains of the fake Tommy Tipp out in the woods on a wheelbarrow. We tried to spread the parts out, not wanting to make a morbid pile of it – birdwatchers and strollers were far more likely to notice a heap, we figured. So we draped his intestines in the branches, planted a foot by some roots, hung his head from the top of a rowan and disposed of his eyes on a pile of rocks. We dug down the soft parts like liver and kidneys, nestled them into moss hollows and leaves. The lungs went out in the brook. It had no heart left to discard, the body of twigs, though that did not surprise me – since the force that had made Tommy Tipp walk and talk had been Pepper-Man all along.

'What an unusual scenery.' My lover looked in on the glen where we had left most of it.

'I just hope no one sees.' I was feeling sick. It was dirty work, messy and ugly, even if I knew what the body really was.

'Tomorrow is a new life,' Pepper-Man said, and didn't know just how right he was about that.

18

In his book, Dr Martin spent a lot of time and pages dwelling on how the Tommy shell fell to pieces. He felt certain it meant something crucial – although, of course, it didn't. The body simply fell apart, that was all.

I remember he asked me about it in a pre-trial session at the hospital. 'Were you angry with Tommy when he couldn't perform?' He had put down his pen, laying it on top of the empty page of his notebook as if sheathing a resting sword. It was a promise, that pen – we were being frank now. Frank and off the record. Just two friends talking, Dr Martin and I. The clock on the wall in our room at the hospital ticked loudly, filling the silence with wasted seconds.

'No, of course not. It was only the Tommy-body coming apart. Pepper-Man performed just fine, as himself.'

'You know it's a very common thing to be upset about, easy to take personally, especially when one's husband has a history of infidelity.'

'I didn't, though. I knew that it wasn't.'

'It's not so common, perhaps, to *get rid* of one's husband when he's "broken".' His eyes twinkled with humor to take the harsh edge off his words. 'Most people just settle for divorce.'

'He was falling apart, what could I do?'

'Marriage counseling, perhaps? Or you could search for a medical solution.'

'He was broken,' I repeated. 'There was nothing to be done.'

'You fell out of love with him?'

'Fell out of love with Pepper-Man?' I blinked at him.

'No, Cassie, fell out of love with *Tommy Tipp*. That would ruin a man for you too, don't you think? Make him "broken" if only metaphorically, if he didn't make you feel the same way as before.'

'I didn't fall out of love with Tommy Tipp. Tommy Tipp was already dead—'

'Or maybe – if he suddenly changed, or even reverted, turned into a man who was different from the one you married and made promises to keep. That is a way of "falling apart" too, if his personality or loyalty disintegrated somehow.'

'I don't know why you keep asking me these questions. I have told you already what happened. The magic was up, the spell was broken.'

'Many married women feel that way, but they don't necessarily decorate the trees with their spouses' body parts.'

'It was only natural that he went back to the woods that he came from.'

'Twigs and leaves?'

'Moss and stones.'

'They didn't find his heart, though.'

'I told you already, Pepper-Man ate it.'

'They are still searching, you know. What would you do if they found Tommy's heart?'

'They won't.'

'But if they did, would you still say that Pepper-Man ate it?'

'I would say that Pepper-Man made it for some reason, for the police to find, perhaps. Made it from a birch root, or a paw.'

'But the body would still not be Tommy Tipp?'

'No.'

'Just a creature you made?'

'A shell of twigs, yes.'

'And nothing they find out there can change your mind?'

'No. I *know* what happened.'

But I was the only one who did – and no one seemed to believe me.

***

And despite our confidence when we wheeled the remains into the woods, I didn't even have time to report Tommy missing before the mushroom hunters had found the body.

The two middle-aged ladies were quite hysterical, and very graphic in their descriptions to the press: *Macabre feast in the woods!* sounded one headline . . . *Body parts hung as garlands* . . . We never saw that coming, to be honest. I was quite unprepared for it all.

I am sure you have seen it for yourselves, on yellowing pages with faded ink. *Wife suspected of murder known to be very jealous* . . . *She was talking to the devil in class, former classmate says* . . . They tell a story that people were more than happy to believe. The whole affair shed some limelight, too, on those in S— who wanted to seek it. Tommy Tipp's old lovers came forth, always anonymous with blurred photos, and so did other people that I'd had the poor fortune to associate with. Our neighbors turned against me overnight, shaking their heads and muttering about 'poor Tommy'. 'We always knew that girl was bad,' they said when asked. 'Always knew she was a little "out there" – never thought it was *this* bad, though . . .'

And there I was, knowing it all to be a lie, and in my fear and confusion I told it like it was, and begged them all to believe me.

Except for that incident with Tommy thirteen years before, I was hardly a murderer. I was a normal housewife.

I have no idea why the detectives claimed to have found Tommy's blood in the basement. I have no recollection of Pepper-Man ever bleeding down there. Maybe he had cut himself repairing something – he was less graceful when wearing human hands. It could have been when we moved all those crates the year before, lots of hauling and carrying then; he could have nicked himself on a splinter or scratched his skin on the wall.

At the very least, the blood couldn't have been found in the amounts they were saying. I think the whole thing was a set-up from the start, they wanted someone to blame, and the one they chose to put it on was me.

POLICE REPORT

Reporting Officer: William Parks
Incident Type: Murder/mutilation of body
Address of Occurrence: Wooded area west of
  S—
Witnesses:
  Elspeth Gordon, 53, female
  Connie Rasch, 54, female
Evidence:
  Golden wedding band with inscription, 'Your
Cassandra Forever', found on tree stump.
  Narrow tire tracks in the mud, 2.5 inches thick.
Weapon/Objects Used: None found at the scene.

At approx. 6 AM the S— Police Department received
a phone call from Mrs Elspeth Gordon. Mrs Gordon
reported seeing the remains of what she assumed
was a man in the woods four miles west of S—.
Mrs Gordon and her visiting friend, Mrs Connie
Rasch, had been in the area looking for mushrooms when they made the discovery.

Officer William Parks and Officer Oswald
Peterson drove out to the area and met the distressed women on a nearby parking lot used by
hikers. Mrs Gordon led the officers to an open
glen, where the body was collected from several
different locations. The deceased's remains were
found on the ground, in eleven different piles
or arrangements, in the trees in six different
arrangements (see attached photos). The officers
agreed that the body was likely a male, judging
from the size of the various body parts. Upon
closer inspection, a head was finally found just
beyond the clearing, near a tree stump. A wedding
band was located on top of the stump. Officer
Parks was then able to make a preliminary

identification of the body as that of Thomas Tipp, age 38, citizen of S—.

The officers at this point called for backup and taped off the area. Officer Peterson went back to the car with the witness to retrieve a camera and protective gear, as some of the matter in the trees was still dripping. Officer Parks stayed behind to guard the area. The witnesses were sent in their own car to the station to give their statements there.

After approx. 30 minutes, backup (Officer Ling and Officer Jenkins) arrived with an ambulance and plastic crates for the remains. Officer Parks was asked via radio to go to Thomas Tipp's residence to make sure his wife was safe and unharmed. Although the identity of the body had not been confirmed yet, it was certain enough that this precaution seemed imperative, especially since Mrs Tipp did not answer the phone.

Officer Parks arrived at Thomas Tipp's residence at approx. 8:45 AM. Cassandra Tipp was at home and seemed to be in high spirits. When asked about her husband's whereabouts, she seemed vague, however, and wondered whether he perhaps was on a fishing trip with his father and had left before she woke. Since there was no suspect in the case, Officer Parks told Mrs Tipp there had been a discovery of a body in the woods, since he worried that she too might be in danger. Mrs Tipp then became quite erratic and repeatedly told the officer that they didn't need to concern themselves: 'There is no body, it's just a shell! There is no body, it's just a shell!' When asked to explain this statement, Mrs Tipp told the officer that her husband was not a man at all but made of twigs and moss.

Officer Parks then called the paramedics.

19

Well, Janus and Penelope – I'm thinking you imagined more drama, more heated feelings and passionate slashes; a crime of jealousy and rage – Aunt Cassie on a psychotic break.

Especially knowing what you do about those other deaths – or think you do. The things Olivia has told you – the reason why our little family is even smaller, now.

That's not how it was, though, was not how it happened. I was never crazed – nor ill.

Tommy Tipp's second death was inelegant and crude, but it was not a murder. It was merely the result of my worlds colliding, human frailty, and the impact this all had on both sides. It was an issue that refused to resolve itself, a wrinkle that wouldn't be ironed. I can't even blame anybody involved, they all just see one side of the coin. Pepper-Man cannot, despite his years as Tommy Tipp, quite relate to human rules.

What is the justice system to him, or anyone who lives for a thousand years? How could he properly assess the risks and see the potential consequences for me? My lawyer, Myra Barnes, and Dr Martin could only see the illusions Pepper-Man and I spun. I know one thing, though: it's hard having your future hanging in the balance, not knowing what other people will decide about your fate. I had already escaped it once, you know, when I made up that life with Tommy Tipp

153

in the brown house, fooling everyone into believing I had bent my head and abided by society's rules. Now I was back at square one again, with the good people of S— defining my worth and my measure, deciding where to put me so that I'd make sense.

***

I will never forget that corpulent, ugly prosecutor, Mr Carew, pacing the courtroom floor, painting a picture for the jury to see of an unhinged, jealous wife who dismembered her husband's body and left it out for the birds to find.

'Imagine her,' he said, 'pulling the body across the floor and down those concrete steps. His head is lolling; his limbs are flailing, as she drags him down to the cold basement. There' – he paused to take a breath – 'she hauls him onto the workbench and gets to it with knives, axe, and cleaver, neatly dismembering him at the joints. Does she cry? No. She is still filled with a raging jealousy. She thinks Tommy's erectile problems stem from his countless affairs. To her, the dismemberment and desecration of the body is just a part of the punishment . . .'

Dr Martin defended me the best that he could: 'She is sick,' he said. 'She has been suffering from delusions since she was a child. You cannot hold her accountable for this crime. In her mind he was not a man at all, but a creature made from natural debris, collected from the woods where she spent her happiest hours as a child.'

In the end, Myra Barnes was the most convincing. She looked like an expensive stick of cinnamon in there; all dressed in brown; tall, powerful, tough and pencil thin. Her hair was a shock of brown curls, sprouting in every direction. She spoke with confidence, knowing she had the support of her expert witness: 'There is no way a woman Cassie's size can move a body the size of Tommy Tipp downstairs to the basement, effectively dismember it, and move it back upstairs to spread it across the forest. If she was involved, she would have needed help, and Cassie doesn't have any friends – we know that from all we have learned in here. Furthermore, there is absolutely no evidence to suggest that she was in any way recruiting outside help for the grisly endeavor. Is Cassie sick? Maybe. Is Cassie jealous? Maybe. Did she kill Tommy Tipp? Hardly. It's much more reasonable to look to Tommy's own criminal past and the "friends" he made back then. Maybe he owed someone money? Maybe he still had a secret life? We don't know that for sure . . .'

Whatever she did, my lawyer convinced them all, wrapped them in doubt and reasoning, and I will forever be grateful for that.

I walked out of there as a free woman, with nothing more than the usual distrust and suspicion tainting my name.

Dr Martin was happy for me, but sad too:

'I guess there is no way I can convince you to commit your-self to a hospital now?'

'No,' I said, bursting with joy. 'No chance at all, my dear doctor.'

***

The transition from the hospital wasn't all painless. On that first day, I paid the taxi driver, dropped my bag in the living room, and set about searching the house for my Pepper-Man, but he wasn't there. Why would he be, anyway? He was done playing Tommy Tipp, and I hadn't been home for ages. But I had been worrying about him, wondering how he was to feed while I was away? I imagined all kinds of things; saw him per-ish among the coiling roots; dried up and shriveled like a mummy; or deserting me for a handsome stag, entwining that life with his instead . . . I was usually able to calm myself down by reminding myself that Pepper-Man had survived long before me and was in every way capable of taking care of himself, and should he choose to leave me for another life, well – there wasn't really much I could do about that.

I didn't dwell on these thoughts for long, though; since building a bond like ours, borne first of need and then sewn up with trust, takes time. I didn't really think my absence for a few months was enough to break us apart. I was still worried I'd find him changed, though – I knew that *I* had changed a bit while I was gone. I had gained weight for once, despite the measly hospital food. I had hips for real, and sizable breasts. My skin color was better too, and I was far less prone to head-aches and fatigues. The nurse who did my blood work at the hospital even mentioned it to me, how my vitamin B deficiency seemed to be suddenly gone, and the iron levels were rising. It was the upside of being without him, I suppose.

Physical Cassie had flourished, while the emotional Cassie ached.

When Pepper-Man was nowhere to be found in the brown house, I set out into the woods to look for him and hoping to see Mara. I walked and I walked, but the path never forked, and the in-between place never came. The veil itself appeared to be gone. I will never forget the horror of that moment, when I thought that my child – my only true home – was lost to me. At first, I convinced myself I had done something wrong, taken a wrong turn, and so went back to the edge of the woods to start fresh. I walked the path, waiting for the bend that sig-naled that the fork was straight ahead, but it never came. Then I screamed and thrashed, and walked around in circles, calling for my loved ones all night. Finally I went home, teary-eyed and weary, voice hoarse. My palms were grimy from hitting tree trunks and pulling moss from the ground, my knees were scabbed from kneeling on the rocky embankment by the brook. My heart felt so empty, as if all feelings had fled.

I felt so fragile in that moment; made of rice paper, so very crisp and thin, just a spark would be enough to set me ablaze and erase everything within. Paper lungs and paper kidneys, paper heart and paper brain. Wind could sweep me off my feet, water could dissolve me. I think I *wanted* to be gone in that moment, sitting there in my empty house, on the cozy blue couch, staring out in the air. No Pepper-Man was there, no Mara . . .

Just me.

I brushed my teeth automatically and pulled on a clean nightgown. I looked into my bag of toiletries, stuffed to the brim with prescription drugs. I was long overdue with the big and blue ones, soon to be overdue with the white and bitter. I took them all out and threw them in the bin.

The last thing I did before I went to bed was to pause by the basement door, where I tore the hateful yellow police tape away.

The brown house was mine again, but the bed was empty. Empty and cold, like me.

When I finally slept, exhausted from my wild search, it was a light and dreamless slumber. No woods, no roots, no Pepper-Man in it. Not even a glimpse of my daughter's chestnut tresses.

The next day started out in the same way: I was all alone. I had barely pulled clothes on and put up my hair when I set out again, searching the woods. When the path still refused to reveal itself, I tried all the tricks I could think of: I walked widdershins around an ancient oak, built circles of stones with incantations; I burned bundles of oak and thorn, and drank teas from wild herbs and flowers. Nothing helped. Faerie was still closed to me. I cried and I wished. I cut myself and let the water in the brook lick the blood from my skin. I pleaded with Pepper-Man to please let me in. I called for Mara, screamed for her.

Still I got no answer.

When I came home again, dawn was nearly there, coloring the sky in a bleak, white light. I went to the bathroom and into the shower, stood there for a while to let the warm water soften my aching limbs. I cried again, for all that I had lost. Tears and snot ran off my face and into the drain while I slowly began to wash myself. It was then that I saw it, through the transparent plastic curtain, a swirl in the mist from the water and the heat. It was not exactly a man, but a shape; a hand, maybe, moving in the fog. Something that could be the outline of a face, eyes in there too, a pair of dark hollows.

I took heart then and swallowed all my doubts, chose to believe that what I'd seen was a sign; that the Otherworld wasn't all lost to me after all, and that maybe one day I would see them again, my Pepper-Man and my Mara. Suddenly, I was laughing instead of crying, standing there in the shower, while the water from the showerhead slowly went from warm to cold and the mist in the bathroom was no more.

When I woke up the next day, long past noon, Pepper-Man was there.

He was sitting on top of the chest of drawers watching me. He looked just like before – when we were married – with his slanted green eyes and chiseled cheekbones, broad shoulders and narrow hips. His hair, which had gradually turned a soft shade of brown, was pooling down in his lap, though it looked more knotted than usual. Relief flooded me and nearly had me in tears again, but then Pepper-Man saw that I was awake and jumped down on the floor.

'So you *can* see me now? I thought we would have to do this for weeks, running about in the woods, screaming and shouting—'

I couldn't help but laugh, even if I was crying. 'I thought I had lost you for good. You and Mara both.'

'They poisoned you against me,' he raged. 'They rose walls between us, lacing your veins with toxins – can you feel it? Feel it slithering through you like a snake?'

'Are you talking about the pills they gave me?' It had never even occurred to me that they would have any effect on my ability to see faeries, even though Dr Martin had told me that was the very point.

'Of course,' said Pepper-Man, 'they are weapons meant to blind you.'

'I didn't think that was possible.'

'Well, now you do.'

'I threw them all away yesterday.'

'Good riddance, then,' he huffed.

'I thought they only worked on crazy people—'

'Well, women like you, running with faeries, *are* crazy – whatever that means.'

'Then I'd rather be the crazy one.' I stifled a fresh bout of tears.

He kissed my head then, lay down with me on the bed – the very same bed we had shared while living together as husband and wife. 'Do you remember how I told you that everything in nature can be eaten by something? Your pills are nature too; those concoctions that you swallow can eat everything faerie. Do not let them feed you those things again.'

'I won't.' I laced my fingers in his hair, was so grateful in that moment just to have him back beside me, I didn't even mind if he scolded me a bit.

'We ran with you last night, Mara and I, and Harriet too, answering your calls and your summons. The gates to the mound stood open wide, and the water girls licked the blood from your skin, and yet you could not see us. Mara was quite distressed, Gwen had to brew her a calming draught and send her to sleep in the yew tree. It is a dangerous power, the one your Dr Martin wields, that can make a mother blind to her child.'

'I don't think he believes himself to be particularly powerful.'

'Even more reason to be scared, then. A sorcerer with no understanding of his craft can do great damage.'

'But I'm here now,' I said, 'and the drugs are wearing off. Come and feast.' I pushed the laces of the nightgown away from my neck, lay back, and closed my eyes.

Home at last.

Later that same day I saw Mara. My girl was waiting for me by the edge of the woods, curly hair wild down her back. I cannot describe the joy I felt, holding her in my arms. My beautiful shadow child, for a brief moment lost to me. She kissed me and hugged me and took me by the hand, led me with her into the woods, into the mound where I told her all that had happened; every accusation and every insult, every nasty headline. All my anger came pouring out of me, even the anger I nourished for my family and long kept suppressed.

In hindsight, I should maybe not have done that – but you must understand that I had no idea what she could do.

What damage she would wreak later on.

**

Your mother did an interview with the *S— Gazette* shortly after I came back from my undeserved stint in the hospital. She felt she had to, I suppose, to save face, or to rescue whatever was left of her dignity after I had so rudely spoiled it. This was before *Away with the Fairies: A Study in Trauma-Induced Psychosis*, mind you. There was no coming back after that.

Mara read it aloud to me, all those pretty things Olivia said. '*We always believed in her innocence,*' she read with a sneer on her face. '*My sister is incapable of violence like that . . .*' Mara took a cinnamon bun from the tray on the table and munched on it while scanning the page, frowning as she did. Marveling, perhaps, at the praise from an aunt who had never showed her mother much warmth before.

I, for one, was happy. 'Maybe she wants us to reconcile,' I suggested. 'Maybe our differences are all in the past.' And in that moment, I truly believed it. So I guess you can imagine my surprise, then, when days went by after I'd returned from the hospital without so much as a word from my sister. I even tried to call her – twice, leaving messages with your help. Olivia never called me back, though, nor did I hear anything from Mother, but that was of course to be expected. Ferdinand came by the brown house one time, standing pale and uncomfortable at the door, refusing to come inside.

'I am glad you are free, Cassie,' he said.

'Well, thank you, Ferdinand,' said I. 'To tell you the truth, so am I.'

**

I have sometimes wondered what would have happened if I had insisted on him coming inside that day. If I had served him coffee or a cup of tea and taken the time to speak with him – would it have changed what happened later? If I had somehow made him feel less alone, less burdened with guilt, could the later disaster have been avoided?

Mara says no, and Pepper-Man too, but I just can't help but wonder.

He was always such a gentle soul, my brother, so easy to lead astray. Maybe I could have saved him.

Maybe it was already too late.

20

It was never easy raising a child of the mound, I want you both to know that. Even before the controversy with Dr Martin's book, there were issues.

The first big obstacle was my age. I was fourteen when I had Mara, and wasn't free to come and go as I pleased. I had school and chores; a different life. I was also horribly unprepared for what motherhood was, not only for the responsibility and the amount of work it would take raising her from that little thing she was at first, but for the onslaught of love that came with it. There was a new moon and a new star on my horizon; a new sun to drizzle gold, and sometimes fire, on my days. Maybe if I had been an older woman I would have seen that coming – but as it was, I didn't. I never knew how much that child would mean to me.

Every day after school, I set out into the woods, heart aching with longing and worry for the day I'd missed. Had she slept all right? Had she cried for me? Were her gums still itching from teething? How much had she eaten – and *what* had she eaten?

They say it takes a village to raise a child. I will forever be grateful to the mound that raised mine. Not only did the faeries feed and shelter her, they cared for her and protected her – treated her like one of their own. They taught her to fend for herself, catch fish with her hands, set snares and call birds, sing life from a tree and into a fox, spin stories and spin them all over again, dance winter in and summer out, walk three times around the mound. Sometimes I would bring her gifts from *my* world, toys I might have treasured myself as a child – china dolls with painted lips; stuffed animals with soft fur; flowery tea sets and coloring books – but she would always prefer the toys from the mound. Pepper-Man made *her* gifts, then: boats of bark and wood to send spinning down the brook, loaded with leaves and acorns, soldiers of twigs and thorns who fought each other on the mossy ground till it ran red with sap of yew, animals carved from teeth and bone where you could still feel life vibrating within them. He made her fans of feathers to wear in her hair, dresses of hide and scarves of down.

She was always Pepper-Man's daughter – not Pepper-Man's daughter at all.

Had he not taken such good care of her, I think I'd have spent the rest of my youth in constant worry. I hated being separated from her, never truly let out my breath as I went through my days, but I knew Pepper-Man cared for her, and that they spoke of me often in the mound. I knew that Harriet fed her blood and cakes, knew Gwen taught her how to shoot with bow and arrows. Francis took good care of her too, teaching her how to play the violin. Her education then was vast but unconventional, made her fit for the mound but nowhere else. She could survive and thrive as a faerie, though she could never live with me. When we found a bird's nest full of screaming pink fledglings, she put them in her mouth and chewed until the screaming stopped. When we came across a rabbit who was hurt, my daughter brought out her bone knife and slit its throat, watched calmly until it was dead. She never sought out pain, but she didn't shy from it either. She didn't share my empathy, had never felt vulnerable and soft, had always been hard, quick and able. Fit for the woods, but not for suburbia – or so I thought at the time.

Now I rather think she'd be a good match: a tiger hiding in the buzz from the wasp nest; a raven among the crows. We could have cleaned her up and groomed her hair, put her in a pink dress and sent her to ballet. Pretended she was a tangerine-marzipan girl, not a hard and red-fleshed poison fruit at all. It would have worked just fine, too, for a while.

But then, we had danced in the woods, Mara and I, while Francis played the flute. We sent boatloads of caged dragon-flies down the brook for the water girls to find. We played with shimmering balls of nothing, sending them across the sky. I was a child too, you know, barely sixteen then. She was my dream doll: all mine and beautiful, and growing up so fast. Her white teeth shining, thick hair cascading down her back. And she was always happy too, back when she was little. Her hoarse laughter filled the woods and sent birds flying from the tree-tops, foxes fleeing the burrows. When she was just weaned from my milk, Mara bonded with a hawk she'd seen, sitting in a grove of pines. Pepper-Man was utterly proud of her then, when she called the bird in herself. He was a gorgeous creature, huge and brown. She fed from him for years; flew with him high in the sky. When he was old and couldn't sustain her, she found herself another one, just as big and gorgeous as the first.

My Mara is very partial to hawks.

She has a temper, though, just like her mother. As she grew older, it grew too. The tantrums of childhood were gone and in their place came searing fire.

'She is a warrior, that one,' said Gwen.

'But who will she be fighting?' I asked.

Gwen shrugged, golden eyes gleaming. 'It will come to her, just you see. Strife will always follow the one who knows how to fight.'

I remember feeling uncomfortable from what she said. I never envisioned my girl having to fight, since she had already fought so hard to be born. Like all mothers, I wished for her days to be light and bright, wanted her to smile far more than she cried. Wished for marzipan, not bitter wine.

Of course, we have very little control of such things; our children are who they are, for better or for worse. My daughter flew with hawks and held a warrior's soul, and there was nothing I could do to change that. My measly attempt to tempt her from that path was merely to teach her how to read. I figured it would do her good to learn a little more about people and the world, that there were other ways to think and act. She loved reading from the start, but it only made her brighter, not more compassionate or soft.

It's what you get from letting your child be raised by faeries, they don't become tame, any of them. They yield to the drums and the pipes; hallow the moon and the night. All life is sacred because they must have it. Blood, birch, and bone. Water, roots, and stones. No sympathy can grow from those things.

Love, though. Love can still grow.

***

Lately, we have been talking a lot about those times, Pepper-Man and I. Those happy days at the mound when Mara was a girl, and ran through the woods in her dresses of hide. It's a privilege of the sunset years to reminiscence, no one expects you to do much anymore, you are allowed to live in the past – and I do, spend hours on the porch, just talking with my Pepper-Man.

166

Mara is all grown up now, of course, has been so since long before the second death of Tommy Tipp. She takes off for days, hunting with her latest hawk, or creating mischief with Francis. The latter has a knack for it, stirring up trouble. He wants to take a child, she's told me, a new and unspoiled child for the mound. Means to make it himself, in the belly of a woman. Means to raise it as his own, just like Pepper-Man did.

'It's such a horribly male thing,' I said while watching the bleeding sunset, 'that need to reproduce to prove one's worth.' I have taken up knitting in my old days, to keep my typing fingers spry, and the needles were clicking merrily while we spoke.

'I do not believe it is particular for males. I think the need disregards both gender and species.' Pepper-Man has been wearing a uniform lately, a faded blue one with shiny buttons, complete with a bayonet. I'm not sure if he knows it himself, that he has donned these new colors. I'm thinking it's an echo from his past, from way back then when he was alive. I could be wrong, of course, it could just as well be that I have warfare on my mind. He is what he eats – always was. Maybe it is my death greeting me, dressing my lover in a soldier's guise.

'Whatever the reason, I would rather not see her entangled in a scheme like that. It's not an easy thing, growing up between the worlds. She of all should know that.'

'I do not believe she thinks of such things. Our daughter is not a creature of compassion.'

'No,' I agreed. 'She is many things, but neither tender nor soft.'

And that, I believe, is what caused all the problems.

***

We are entering murky waters now. We are close to the parts that concern you the most. We shall speak of the events that pierced your childish contentment and ruptured your lives. The things that have haunted you ever since.

We are nearing the end of the family Thorn.

21

We had good years, Pepper-Man and I, in the house you are standing in now. Mara too, when she wanted to. Since we moved further away from town, she was always welcome inside, but she is partial to the mound, my daughter, was born there, after all. Is a wild thing, always was. Just like Faerie.

It was here in the lilac house I flourished as a writer. The closeness to the mound was good for me, the closeness to my Mara. Money came trickling in even after Dr Martin's 'Cassie fund' dried up.

Book money. Faerie money. Blood money.

All of which you are soon to have – if you only read a little further.

I spent years making this house what it is today; lived with carpenters, painters, and their rubble and tools. I ordered furniture and had strong men in overalls carry it inside. It was quite splendid in its prime, but as all things built on faerie land, the woods will always creep in and settle, line the bottoms of your shelves. What you see as decay is merely the woods taking back what once belonged to them.

We are just guests here, on this land – there will always be fungus in your bathtub, ants in your tea, and squirrels on your porch. Faerie woods are wild lands. Everything grows faster, higher. Everything is driven by an insatiable appetite, a hunger for life, hunger for living. In this, the lilac house is just an island. There is no point in trying to keep it neat.

***

I want you to know that I *do* know my facts from fiction. I would be a poor writer if I didn't. I know that Ada in my first novel never went to Honolulu. I know that Ellie in my next one never fell in love with her sister's widower. I know that Laura in my most recent novel, which was probably my last, never opened a hair salon and moved in with the janitor next door. I know that never happened. I know it never will. I have never had conversations with my characters; never dreamt of them at night. They are just images, pretend-people that my readers can relate to. My books are just me taking a sip of fairyland magic and running with it, spinning it, spooling out a story.

The faeries love my stories, just because of that humanity. To them, they are glimpses into our world, into the minds, hopes, and dreams of people still alive. They are also a payment for the faerie jars themselves. They give me inspiration and I bring them dreams. That is how such bargains have always worked – we sate each other's hunger. Pepper-Man takes life from me, but gives me life as well. The faerie jars are a part of that life, and Mara is another. Tommy Tipp, or at least the wicker version that we made to save me, was a part of my faerie bargain, too.

But the regular readers, too, love my stories. At first it was morbid fascination, I think, that drew them to the shelves and made them pick up my little pink book. I had kept my married name, of course, and it was proudly displayed on the cover in golden letters with curlicues:

Golden Suns by Cassandra Tipp.

I was so proud of that book. The first one of many, as it turned out.

Later, when the memory of the trial and Dr Martin's book had faded, I became the sad widow who worked through her grief and family tragedy by writing about love and happy ever afters. They thought it was beautiful then, my readers, beautiful and romantic that I wrote of such things after having lost my one and only.

Mostly, though, it was habit that made my readers come back. They do that, you know, if you tell a good story. They crave more of that same feeling you gave them, want to immerse themselves in your waters again, swim deep in your lagoons and drink from that same well. I gave them a good swim forty-two times. You can count them all on that shelf in the parlor. Every one of them was fueled by a set of faerie jars; grown from rabbit's teeth, flower buds, and leaves. I have read them all out loud in the mound, too, with golden eyes peering at me, the heat from the hearth licking my back. I received cakes and wine for my trouble, followed by ever more exquisite jars to quench my literary thirst.

But Dr Martin was gone by the time *Golden Suns* hit the shelves.

Only four years after he published *Away with the Fairies: A Study in Trauma-Induced Psychosis*, he died quietly in his bed. 'Natural causes', as they say, though I had my own thoughts about that.

***

I have often wondered what he'd make of all this, the success that I've become. He, who wanted to commit me to a hospital and have me chew pills and get shots forevermore. Not out of some ill intent, but because to him, as much as he loved me, I was still his patient.

The first time I saw a Japanese translation of *Golden Suns*, I pretended he was there with me, his hand resting on my shoulder, and he said:

'Look at that, Cassie. I can see that I was wrong. You really have a purpose to fulfill in this world. It would have been a terrible mistake if you spent your life in a hospital.'

But that was just wishful thinking, mind you. I know that it wasn't real.

***

Mara was never fond of Dr Martin. To her he would always be the man who tried to take me away.

I had taught her to read, and she read a lot, and read his book too, shortly before he died.

I don't know what she had expected it to be – perhaps another faerie mound fantasy, or the adventures of her mother, rescued by the woods – but of course, it was not a happy story, it was gritty and harsh, littered with medical terms and regrets.

It left me little credit, truth be told.

'It says in here that you are making me up,' she confronted me one day. I was in the kitchen, making a pie.

'It is just what Dr Martin thinks, it doesn't mean anything,' I said. 'You know how it is with faeries and humans. You are the *hidden* people, after all, and should stay that way, too, for many reasons.' A lesson I myself should have taken to heart a very long time ago.

'But he is spreading these lies to the world,' she said. 'He makes you sound stupid, or insane.'

'They aren't really lies when he thinks they are true. For him I suppose I *am* quite insane.'

'But how can he be so sure you are making us up – has he ever *seen* a faerie?'

'No, my sweet, I think that is the point.' I wiped the flour off my hands on the apron. 'People who don't believe in faeries have usually never met one.'

'But people believe in a lot of things they have never seen, like black holes or deep water fish.'

'That is easier to prove, although I don't think everyone believes in black holes. For many people that's just a story, too, being so very far off as to be unreal.'

'I still don't think it is right, though, him talking about you like this, for money.'

'The money from that book got us this house.' I bent down to check on the pie. 'Dr Martin and I agree to disagree,' I said while I rose back up. 'I leave him to his convictions, he leaves me to mine.'

'But he doesn't,' she argued. 'He wanted to treat you with pills, it says so here in the book, and it says other things too, about me . . . and my father.'

'I think we should leave that alone.' I turned my back on her, unable to meet her eyes. I busied my hands cleaning the kitchen counter, wishing against all odds she would leave the matter be. She was all grown up by then, though. I couldn't forbid her anything. I couldn't protect her from going where she shouldn't.

'But is it true, Mother?' she asked. 'Did you suffer like that when you were a child? Am I a daughter of your pain . . . ? Did you take me to the mound to bury me there?' Her voice rose behind me.

'Of course not, Mara, of course not.' I spun around and placed my arms on her shoulders, made to pull her into my embrace. She wouldn't have it, though, and forced my arms away. 'I brought you to the mound so that you could *live*,' I told her, standing before her. 'You are a child of Faerie. You have always been a child of Faerie.'

'But Faerie is the opposite of life, isn't it?'

'No – not quite.'

'But why would you even have me live, then?' Her voice broke and she looked utterly crushed. My heart ached, bled salt. 'If my beginning was like it says in the book? Why didn't you just let me die? You were so young and so broken. So sad and so alone—'

'So I wouldn't be,' I interrupted her. 'I wouldn't be sad and alone if I had *you*. You were always mine, you see, ever since you were the size of a finger, sleeping on an oak leaf in Harriet's palm, and before that too, you were mine. I will never regret having you.'

'But those who hurt you so, will you ever make them pay?'

'Whatever good would come of that?'

'I don't believe in letting the world deal its blows, I believe in fighting back.'

'For what, Mara? Fight for what?'

'For justice and pride . . . for your dignity.'

'Nothing good ever comes from any of those things – what is justice, anyway? What is pride or dignity? It doesn't matter, Mara, none of it does. I survived. That is all.'

'So it *is* true, then, what he says?'

'Well, the "trauma" in the title does come from a place, but everything is very confusing . . . I don't really know what had happened back then—'

'Seems from what he wrote that you deserve a lot more in this life than to merely survive.'

'Why? I have it all: a beautiful daughter, a wonderful home . . .' Suddenly she'd made me feel so small, like the tiniest of mice living under the floorboards. Made me feel like I should have taken up arms, not kept my head low and pretend it didn't blow. Your children can do that, make you feel that shame. 'I let him write that book.' I defended my lack of courage. 'I let him tell the story there.'

'But it is *his* story about you, not your own.'

'Still,' I shrugged. 'And remember, Mara, some of it is true, but some of it is not. There are certainly a lot of things that never happened in there, too. It's all just so horribly mixed up.'

'But you let your family rage at you and cast you aside. You let them say that it is *all* lies, let them live in such denial—'

'I don't know that they could be blamed—'

'I understand that you are hurting, Mother, maybe too much to fight and burn, but *I* will fight this one for you. For your sake and for mine.'

My blood ran cold in my veins. 'No, please, Mara, I wish you wouldn't.' Why poke at a resting bear?

She lifted her chin up high, eyes glowing like crushed embers. 'If I don't, who will?'

'It was all such a long time ago, they are so old now, they will soon die—'

'And never have to pay?'

'Yes, just that. Let there be peace now. That is all I want from life.'

'You are growing old.' Her eyes narrowed to slits. 'Only old people say such things. People with no hope left. People who have given in.'

'Maybe I have.' I shrugged again. 'And maybe it is enough to have survived.'

22

We keep coming back to it, don't we? That book that he wrote. *Away with the Fairies: A Study in Trauma-Induced Psychosis.* Maybe because it played such a crucial role in everything that happened later. It changed the course of fate, I think. Changed us all.

The book itself is rather dry. It recounts Dr Martin's relationship with a young female patient, thinly disguised as 'C—', who later went on to face murder charges. Dr Martin writes about a troubled young girl who has lost her ability to tell reality from fantasy. His theory is that she had been a victim of sexual and emotional abuse from a very early age, and had constructed a world of her own to escape to. The real problems begin when her fantasy world spills into the real world, confusing the two in her mind. *She is living in both worlds at the same time. Her fairy friends are as real to her as her family and schoolmates. Maybe even* more *real.* He used Pepper-Man as an example of how 'C—'s' imaginary world evolves: *She is attempting to heal herself by altering her cast: the kindly monster from her childhood (her abuser), who gives her gifts, but also hurts her, is transformed into a prince in her adolescence. He becomes a beautiful savior who has come to take her away from her cruel family. His counterpart in reality then becomes the man who would be her husband. Even though it seems irrational for healthy people, this attempted healing is actually a sign of a highly functioning survival instinct. Her mind is struggling to heal the wounds inflicted on her by rewriting the story and erasing the things that hurt.*

As stories go, his is not a bad one. Dr Martin had taken it all and managed to wrap it all up in one neat little bundle. Applied his magnifying glass to it and knitted a new narrative from the bits and bobs. About Mara, he said: *The abortion was another violation of her body, another situation in which she was completely helpless and at the mercy of her abusers. Her mind gets to work and unravels the incident and lets her write a new one, in which she saves the child by taking it to the fairy mound (where the dead still live). The child is lost in the real world, but lives on in her fantasy land. She copes with her loss by not coping at all because she does not have to. The child is still there, only displaced – allowed to grow up in a way that C— had not been able to do.*

No wonder Mara was upset, poor child.

He spends quite some time searching for the origins for my 'delusions', examining everything from the fairytale books I had as a child, to the selection of books on folklore and myths available at the S— library at the time. It's unclear if he was satisfied with his search.

He doesn't say right out that 'C—' had in fact killed her husband, but notes: *If she had murdered her spouse as the result of a lovers' quarrel or a relationship grown stale, her mind would have quickly been at it again, rewriting the story to heal the wounds. Maybe he had not been human at all, but a man made from twigs and river stones? Maybe the real prince had been hiding inside him, and the body in question, with its flaws and appetites, didn't truly matter? Maybe, as her mind keeps justifying*

her deeds, the real husband has been dead all along, and it is her
fairy consort, her childhood solace, who has been posing as him for
years? No crime, then, to dismember his body and wheelbarrow the
pieces into the woods . . .

Your mother and grandparents were not pleased by this
book, I can tell you that. Dr Martin's star crash-landed in a pile
of shit in their yard, stinking up the whole neighborhood.

'Where is this coming from?' Mother asked me on the
phone. Screamed at me, really. 'Why these allegations *now*? Is
it because we weren't there at the trial?'

'It's just a book,' I tried to tell her.

'But it's presented as the truth, Cassie. Everyone will read
it. We won't ever recover from this, don't you have any compassion for your mother and father?'

'Not really, no. I haven't seen any of you for a while. Sometimes I forget you're even there.'

'Well, don't you think that we at least deserve a little
respect? Raising you was hard. You were not an easy child—'

'I know, I was *bad*, wasn't I?'

'Yes, you were. You just never could seem to do anything
right – and yes, maybe I was harsh at times, but that doesn't
mean I'm accountable for whatever became of you in life.
What poor choices you made . . .'

I couldn't help but chuckle at her outburst. Which only
enraged her further:

'Stop laughing at me, Cassie! What is this? Your revenge? I
will have you know that you are responsible too, for everything
that happened. Had you only not been so ba—'

I hung up the phone.

I didn't hear her voice again until the funeral.

***

I can imagine it was hard on them. The book caused a lot of stir, and the press was back on my case, following me around and snapping pictures, and taking pictures of my family, too, whenever they dared leave the house. I saw a picture of Mother once, on the front page of a newspaper, her head wrapped in a scarf, large Hollywood sunglasses. Olivia, too, wore hats, broad brimmed and heavy with ornamental flowers and bows.

I always refused interviews. I couldn't stomach talking about it and wanted to keep my mock anonymity intact. Dr Martin did a few TV shows, though, where he discussed 'C—' at length with other doctors and survivors of abuse. In the end I think that book created a little more compassion for people who have been through a lot, and that's worth something, isn't it?

But then there was Mara.

***

I hadn't expected her to react to the book in the way that she did. Hadn't thought it would affect her much at all. She was fiery, of course, had always been that, but I hadn't realized it would cause her such pain.

I even called Dr Martin to warn him about the strength of her feelings:

'She is quite upset,' I told him, 'now that she has read it. She is particularly upset about the story you told of her origins.'

'In what way would you say she is upset, Cassie?' Dr Martin sounded wary on the other end.

'She is blaming me for not taking my revenge. She says that she will do it for me.'

'Cassie, I want you to take a deep breath and prod a bit inside yourself . . . Do you *share* Mara's feelings?'

'No,' I said at once. 'I don't think it happened that way at all.'

'But you do, don't you? You know what I wrote is true.'

'Truth-shmuth . . .'

'*Cassie* . . .'

'I'm sorry – I'm just trying to do what you say and prod my insides, but these are all just Mara's feelings, not something that we share. I even feel a bit guilty – I admit – for *not* sharing them.'

'How come?'

'Well, it's like she wants something from me, wants me to *blaze* like she does, and that I should be ashamed – she thinks me weak for not acting. For not "raising arms", if you see what I mean?'

'But you did that, Cassie. You did fight back, only you did it in your own way, and Mara is proof of that.'

'Because I made her up?'

'Just that. You fought back with the tools you had at your disposal.'

'Somehow I don't think that will do as an explanation to *her*.'

'What do you think she will do, then, with these angry feelings?'

'I don't know, but I'm worried.'

'Maybe you should consider hospital one more time? Or take me up on my offer and accept a prescription—'

'No, Dr Martin. No. I will lose them all, then, and I don't want that.'

'I understand that it's hard to let go, but you wouldn't want Mara to hurt anyone, right?'

'Of course not, that is why I'm calling you – for advice.'

'I am really obligated to tell someone if I think you pose a threat to yourself or someone else, or if I think that Mara does.'

'Do you, though?'

'You certainly have me worried . . .'

I gave a small laugh, insecure and shivering. 'Why do you think she is so mad?' I whispered into the phone.

'Well, I think Mara may be changing just as Pepper-Man did, because you need her to be something else now. Maybe she really is your daughter, in a sense, a part of you that belongs to you but that grows independently, becoming a force to be reckoned with and surprising even you.'

'I am sure she will disagree, but please, go on . . .'

'Maybe Mara is your anger that you never allowed yourself to feel, because you couldn't afford it. You are stronger now, though, the book is out there and thousands of people have read your story. You can *allow* yourself to be angry now, people on TV even *encourage* you to be angry. No harm will come to you for it. Maybe Mara has become the embodiment of that anger.'

'My child of pain?'

'Just that . . .'

'Or just a very angry daughter who has just learned something bad once happened to her mother.'

'That too.'

'So what do I do?'

'You have to find out where her rage is going, if she's a threat to anyone.'

'And if she is?'

'Then you must commit yourself, Cassie, there really is no way around it.'

'How will that help with Mara?'

'Trust me, Cassie. It will.'

***

I never did commit myself to the hospital, though, even after I realized what Mara could – would – do. I knew it wouldn't help one bit. Rather it would make things worse, with me not being there to calm her.

She once said she went to see Dr Martin before he died, but I don't know if it's true or not.

'What did you say to him?' I asked her. We were sitting on my porch, watching the sunset, sharing a jar of faerie tea between us. The very same jar that became the beginning of *Golden Suns.*

'At first I didn't say much at all. He was in his office, typing, and I just stood there in the corner where the light didn't reach and watched him.'

'That was not very kind of you. You know how people hate being watched from the shadows.'

'Well, I wanted to see him.'

'And then what? What happened?'

'He coughed a bit, sipped his cocoa . . .'

'And?'

'I went over to him and stood before him, looked him in the eyes when he raised his head. He made a sound, the kind they make, like an outburst – or a scream . . .'

'He was surprised, then?'

'Of course. Then I said, real slow, so that I knew that he heard every word: "Now you have seen a faerie." '

'You didn't.'

'Of course I did.'

'And did he really see you?'

'Of course he did.'

'What did he say?'

'Nothing. I left. I think I scared him. I hope I did.'

'You shouldn't have scared poor Dr Martin.'

'Well, nothing to do for it now.' She sipped her tea. 'With him being dead and all.'

'Yes,' I said, 'such a shame.'

We finished our tea in silence.

23

We have to talk about your uncle, Ferdinand.

24

I don't know how much your mother has shared with you about everything that happened. You were still teens then, fragile saplings with tender hearts, she would have wanted to spare you the details.

Neither do I know how close you were to him, what kind of an uncle he was to you. I was rarely invited to your birthdays, as you know. I never had a natural place at the family table, not even while Tommy Tipp was assumed to be alive.

I am not bitter about that. I want you to know that I wanted it that way.

Back when you were small, Pepper-Man-in-Tommy and I took the easy route and went to see the Tipps rather than the Thorns when Santa came to town. It kept our neighbors and friends from asking, and the Tipps never knew the difference; they thought Pepper-Man was their son all along.

No one ever cared to ask why we so rarely saw *my* family. I have no idea how your mother explained that to you two. She used to bring you to our brown house, though, do you remember? Four times a year, three months apart to the date. I am sure she had it penciled in her calendar: *Take kids to see Aunt Cassie and Uncle Tommy.* You probably don't see it that way, but I think you were fooled by that. I think it was your mother's way of throwing you off the scent. It was the bare minimum she had to do to convince you everything was normal and safe. And if someone asked you, at school or at friends', about us, your aunt and uncle, you could always say: 'We saw Aunt Cassie just recently, her petunias look lovely this year,' or 'Aunt Cassie and Uncle Tommy just bought a new parasol, we had ice cream in the garden, with strawberries.' That way no one would know that our relationship was frigid as a barren nun, and the two of you would grow up with the illusion that you were part of a healthy family.

Suited her, suited me. Suited Mother, I presume.

I think you've been fooled like that often.

The visits stopped, though, after the trial. Despite what she said, Olivia always thought me guilty. I think she worried about letting her chickens near the viper's nest, and I can't really blame her for that. I honestly can't say I've missed you much either. Janus, you were always such a sullen child, always discontent. And you, Penelope, afraid to get your hands dirty, so picky about your sweets: too sour, too sweet, too sticky, too much. I have no patience with things like that.

I don't know how your mother justified it then; how, if ever, she discussed those things with you. If you ever asked: 'Are we going to Aunt Cassie's?' or if you, like me, let out a breath of relief when summer became autumn and autumn became winter without so much as a glimpse of Olivia's car in my drive. I've never really liked children much, except for my own girl, of course. You two are grown now, Penelope child-less, I think you can relate.

Just because I lived so apart from you, I don't know how your uncle was with you. If he was a funny uncle who played with you in the garden after Sunday dinners, a serious uncle you rarely spoke to, an uncle you were afraid of because he snapped and barked, or the kind who made you feel uncomfortable because his jokes weren't really that funny.

I know that, to me, Ferdinand was always more like a shadow; a tall, pale specter that drifted through our childhood home. He didn't say much, never laughed. I always believed that he had a good heart, but I never really examined it. Between his sisters, he disappeared too easily. He was crumbling under Mother's thumb and shivered in my father's fist. I think he spent much of his childhood afraid, worrying about the next day, yet he never moved further away from our shared prison than the house next door, which Mother bought for him when it became clear he did not have the drive to do it himself.

He must have been such a disappointment to her, another one to add to the list. She would never say that, of course, least of all to you, but I can imagine *he* heard it, more than once. She would have tormented him daily with accusations; how his lack of ambition was the end of them, how he never could seem to succeed at anything, how he could have had it all yet there he was, drifting from one useless job to the next, never finishing any of the countless educations he pursued before he gave up and resigned.

You two can never truly relate to that, what it's like being broken. How it is to grow up a white-bellied dove among pitch-black crows, a piece that won't fit the puzzle. You, with your suburban castle childhood home, Miss S— beauty queen mother, and executive father, how could you relate to failure, to being scarred on the inside, bleeding from within?

You can't.

I don't think Ferdinand was always like that, though. I think he could have been a crow like all the rest, a magnificent one too, soaring high. But our brother had that one flaw, the heart that I mentioned. To a boy as soft as he, my family was poison. I'm counting myself in this time, I too was a dose of arsenic lacing that poor boy's veins: too loud, too angry, too wild for him.

We were no fit company for doves.

After I moved to the brown house, I'm sad to say he almost ceased to exist in my mind, became a distant part of Mother, maybe, her silent shadow or willing servant. I remember feeling pity – I do, but never once did I call him or invite him to my home. He was a stranger, this brother of mine, even when we shared a roof.

So imagine my surprise, then, when I found him at my door at the lilac house, red-cheeked and ruffled, pale hair a mess. The navy-blue tie with little golf clubs on it hung like a deflated balloon down his chest. His blue sports jacket was unbuttoned.

This was nearly two years after Dr Martin died. I was nearing my forties then, and looked the part, too. Ferdinand, though, had aged more. He looked as if he were closing in on fifty, with gray temples and sagging skin. I don't know how long he had looked like that before he came to see me.

Maybe it was all that worrying that did it, all that tossing and turning at night. I was unprepared for his visit – any visit – and remember I felt a jolt of anxiety myself when I heard his car park outside.

'You have to help me,' he said when I opened the door. I had thrown on a satin robe over my pajamas. It was way past noon, but you know what it's like, us eccentrics like to lounge about and eat croissants for breakfast.

'Ferdinand, what is it? What has happened, is it Mother?' That was my first thought, that the old witch had finally keeled over, the heart of ice shattering in her chest.

He shook his head, looking miserable, biting his lips, flexing his fists. 'No,' he said in a thin voice, 'it's worse.'

'Come on in, then.' I opened the door for him. He staggered as if drunk, but he didn't smell like alcohol. I placed him by the kitchen table and poured coffee in large pink mugs. Then I sat down across from him, wondered if I should take his hand and then decided to let it be, it would simply be too awkward. Instead, I just sat there and waited for him to speak.

He seemed a little calmer then, cradling his cup, blowing on his coffee, but the eyes he turned to look at me were pained. 'I think I'm losing it, Cassie. I'm really losing it.'

'What has happened?' I curbed another impulse to touch him. 'Why are you so upset? Did Mother do something to you? Did *he*?'

'No . . . no, nothing like that. It's in my mind, Cassie, it's my mind . . .'

'Tell me.' A surge of worry began to grind in the pit of my stomach. This didn't bode well. Not well at all.

He gathered his wits enough to raise his gaze and meet mine. 'I always thought you innocent, you know.'

'I know that,' I said, though I didn't.

'No matter what they said, I never believed it was true. You are not a killer, Cassie. Never were.'

'Why are you bringing this up now?' The worry bloomed and ached.

Ferdinand removed his glasses, dabbed at his eyes with a handkerchief. 'It isn't right,' he said weakly. 'It isn't right to see such things.'

I suddenly felt cold. 'See *what*, Ferdinand? What did you see?'

'Nothing.' He turned his teary eyes up to look at me across the table. 'Nothing for a while—'

'But you did, didn't you? You did see *something*.' My heart was hammering fast in my chest.

His gaze started flickering, from the cupboards to the table and back again. 'I don't know what I saw.'

'Tell me, brother, maybe *I* know.' Suddenly it was the most important thing in the world to have him tell me. To confirm what I suspected.

'It was such a long time ago.'

'Back when we were children? Did you see *him*?'

'Yes. How could I ever forget that thing?'

Suddenly I was furious, wanted to smash my mug into the wall. 'Why didn't you ever tell me? Why didn't you say anything?' Why hadn't he supported me? Verified my stories? Then I felt sad for all the fear he had carried. I knew all too well what that was like.

'I told Father.' His gaze dropped. 'I told Father and I wish I never had . . . I never spoke of it again to anyone and after a while I stopped seeing . . . Then you moved away. But I think of it, often. That creature – his ghastly face looming—'

'Oh, Ferdinand.' Finally I touched him, lay my hand on his. His skin was cold and clammy. 'What happened now? Did you see him again?'

He took a moment, shook his head and swallowed hard. 'Last night, when I was playing the piano, something so strange happened. I had left the patio doors open to let the wind inside. I do that sometimes, so I can feel the night around me while I play.'

'And . . . ?'

'Suddenly I got this feeling like someone was watching me,

and when I looked up, there was a woman there, standing just inside the doors where the draft made the curtains billow.'

'Oh no.' I knew at once who that woman had to be.

'Yes . . . and she looked so strange, but I was too surprised to be really scared at the time. Her hair was all wild and her clothes were old and dirty; long skirts and a cape of hide. She smelled, too, like earth and something bitter, like herbs or sap from needle trees. Her eyes, though, her eyes, they were glowing, Cassie, glowing toward me in the dark . . . There was something familiar about her face, as if I knew her. She looked a little bit like you did before – when you were young.'

'Oh no,' I said again. A pounding pain had appeared at my temples, and the churning knot in my gut exploded. I could only imagine where this was going. 'What did she say to you?'

'Well, when she saw that I was looking at her she crossed the floor and stopped right by the piano. "So you can see me, even uninvited," she said. "Who are you?" I asked her, felt cold to the bone. "I am one of my mother's lies," she replied. Why did she say that, Cassie? What did she mean?'

'I don't know,' I lied, one of my worst. 'Go on . . .'

'Well, she leaned in and I pulled back, and then she said, very slowly, "Never say I wasn't here, my mother's brother," and then she left. Just slipped out the patio doors and was gone.'

'She said that?'

'Yes.' Ferdinand slammed his mug down on the table. 'What did she mean by that? Is it you that she's talking about? Who is she? Some stray you picked up, some fellow patient from the psychiatric ward that felt kinship to you? Her eyes, though, those eyes . . .'

'Who do *you* think she was?'

He shook his head, looked at me with horror and despair. 'I don't know,' he said. 'I don't know.'

'A stray?' I raised my eyebrows. 'A patient?'

'What else could she be?' His voice was thin. 'She couldn't be *it*, could she?'

'*It* as in what? My daughter? A faerie?'

'Don't *say* that!' His whole body began to shiver. 'It's not possible – she couldn't be. Father has forbidden me to speak of it—'

'Has he now?'

'Who is she?' He removed his glasses to dab at his eyes with the handkerchief.

'My daughter, Mara.'

'Mara, huh?' he tested the name. 'Why did she come to me?'

'She has her own reasons, I don't always follow them.'

'Is it her, the daughter in that book?'

'Yes.'

He took a moment, put down the crumpled-up handkerchief and put his glasses back on. 'I always knew Tommy wasn't right. I always knew there was something odd about him. He didn't feel like he was real. It still confuses me that he had everyone fooled.'

'People only see what they want to see.'

'No. Sometimes we just see, and have no choice in the matter.'

'True.'

'But what about those other stories in the book? Mother and Father and—'

'I don't know,' I cut him off. 'It was all very confusing back then. I don't know what really happened and have long since stopped caring.'

'But Father—'

'I don't know. *She* thinks so, Mara does. She is angry with him, so angry . . .'

He sighed deeply, drew a hand across his brow, brushing away stray strands of blond and gray. 'I still have nightmares about him – your Pepper-Man.'

'He isn't so bad. He has changed quite a bit.'

'I only remember him in my dreams – tall and thin and scary, black lips and long nails, clothes all in tatters . . .'

'He had been intimate with a tree for some time.'

'How can you be so flippant about it?' His gaze across the table was imploring.

'Habit,' I shrugged. 'You get used to it.'

'I don't want to get used to it.'

'Of course you don't.'

'It's real, though, isn't it? It's *there*!'

'Yes, it most certainly is there. I've been telling you that for some time now.'

***

Your mother would of course tell you that this kitchen table exchange of ours never happened. She would say that I'm making it all up, because I can. Because Ferdinand is dead and can never say different, and that I'm taking advantage of that.

I can't prove her wrong.

I never recorded my conversations with my brother, and they won't appear in any doctor's notes. All I have is myself and my memory, which Olivia will caution you to doubt.

She will say it never happened.

I will tell you that it did.

That, and all the rest that followed.

Every single thing.

25

I spoke to my daughter about it at length when she came around to see me next. It was a windy day and her skirts were spinning around her ankles when she came in through the door, picking debris from her hair with her fingers.

'You can't go around scaring people like that.' I was sitting on the champagne-colored sofa, pink ink pen in hand, editing my new book. 'Whatever were you trying to accomplish?'

She shrugged. 'I didn't do anything, I just visited, that's all. I didn't *want* him to see and made no effort that he would. He just did.'

'And now he's terrified.' I pushed my purple-rimmed glasses on top of my head.

'Well, I can't do anything about that. I would think you'd be pleased, truth be told. At least now someone knows you were telling the truth all along.'

'It doesn't matter what they think. I don't care if they think I lie. I've been called a liar my whole life, why would it matter to me *now*?'

'Don't you think *he* deserves to know, though? Deserves to know that his sister isn't mad?'

I shrugged. 'I can't see how that would make any difference to Ferdinand. I hardly think he's been lying awake at night pondering the state of my mind.'

'But still, doesn't it make you happy to know that he knows?'

I straightened up on the sofa and put my pen down. 'If Ferdinand had been a bolder man, he would have known all along. He saw Pepper-Man when he was a boy.'

Her eyes widened in surprise. 'Then why didn't he say something?'

'He did – to our father. That was a great mistake.'

'What happened?'

'I don't know exactly, but it wasn't good. He never spoke of it again, decided it wasn't real, I suppose. Decided not to believe.'

'Oh, that man,' she scoffed, plunged down beside me on the sofa, manuscript pages flying. 'Then why was he so surprised to see me, if he knew all along we were real?'

'He doesn't want to believe, and I can't blame him. Look at what happened to me.'

'But still, isn't it good, Mother, to know there is someone else out there who sees?'

I sighed. 'What do you want, Mara, a revolution? For the faeries to rise up and claim their existence? For the veil to come down so you too can all have nice houses and Sunday roasts?'

'I would like to be *real*. I would like to not be a tainted secret, something you have to hide in the mound.'

'I never took you to the mound to hide you.' I picked stray pages from the floor. 'You know how that went.'

'Do I?' Her eyes were gleaming.

'Sure you do.'

'Not according to Dr Martin. According to him, you were driven to a clinic some distance from here and went through surgery to have me removed.'

'Well, you are here, aren't you, so obviously that didn't happen.'

'But if it did—'

'Then it went wrong.'

'That easy?'

'Yes.'

She sat for a moment, mulling it over. 'I don't want a nice house or a Sunday roast—'

'Yes you do. You all want that. You want to live like everyone else. That is the curse of your humanity, that need to join the pack.'

'I am not human,' she argued.

'And yet you are – all of Faerie was, once.'

'Dead, then, and changed, isn't that what you think?'

'Yet you live.'

'On the fringe, far out in the woods; just a shadow passing through your rooms.'

'What do you want, Mara? Truly?'

'For someone to pay for my life.'

'What life?' I was honestly confused.

'Just that, Mother, *what* life? The life I did not live at all or the life that I was given? A life soaked in your blood—'

'But you are happy, Mara, aren't you?' I tried to touch her hair, soothe her in some way, but she brushed my hand aside.

'I will be happy when the debt is paid.'

'Oh, Mara,' I said, 'I am not sure if that is the right approach—'

'What is, then? To be content with what I got, knowing no other life than this, invisible and hungry, living at the edges of people's minds.'

'Well, it *is* life.'

'But *is it*?'

'Sure it is!'

'I am angry,' she said, 'for the injustice of it all. I have paid with my life for someone else's crime—'

'We don't know that for sure.'

'Am I Pepper-Man's daughter?' Her hard gaze turned on me again, smoldering like embers.

'I don't know.' I struggled to meet that gaze. 'You are Pepper-Man's daughter – not Pepper-Man's daughter. Does it matter what you are? You *are*.'

'Oh, Mother.' She leaned back and stretched out her legs. 'You were always such a good victim.'

'I don't think I was, though Dr Martin would say so.'

'Even if the doctor's story isn't true, you were still taken. Pepper-Man took you when you were a child.'

'. . . I came to love him.'

'But did you have choice? What were you to do? Taken into Faerie at such a young age.'

'It is the curse of the sight.'

'It is the curse of a predator falling upon its prey – I should know all about that.'

'He needed to feed—'

'Yes, they all say that.'

'What do you want from me, Mara?' I was nearing my wits' end.

'From you? Nothing. You have bled enough.'

'Why can't you just let it be, then? Let there be peace now and no more grief.'

'I've tried – I can't. You had your choices stolen, and so did I, by extension.'

'We all do, Mara, that's what it's like being born. We can't pick and choose the life we'll live, if we'll grow up in S—, Paris, or New York—'

'But no matter where you live, it's all life, and yours, not borrowed from someone else's blood.'

'The Sunday roast would disagree, don't you think? We all live of *something*. You are a faerie, Mara, with magic at your fingertips, a life beyond measure. Most people would consider that a gift.'

'I don't, though. I consider it a consolation prize.'

I sat quiet for a while. It's always hard for a parent to learn that what you could give has not been enough, that all the hard choices you made mean nothing to the child. That you always gave the wrong thing, thinking it was the right. 'What will you do?'

'What I do best.'

'Leave poor Ferdinand alone,' I begged her. 'He has nothing to do with any of this.'

She didn't listen to me, though.

Of course not.

***

Daughter of pain. Daughter of anger. Daughter of love, too, I always believed.

Where I was soft, she was hard. Where I adapted, she stood firm. It must be hard to burn as bright as that – exhausting, too, I reckon. Where I chose shield, she chose sword. I never looked back, nothing good came from that. Mara, though, she was always looking back, unraveling the story and following the threads until she came back to the beginning, pinning down guilt where she saw fit. She was never content with just living – or not, depending on the side of the coin.

***

I will give you a way out, Penelope and Janus, you can still walk away from this. You can abandon the story before it gets ugly. The password is THORN, yes, THORN, like my maiden name. But then again, you don't know that for sure. I can still change my mind on the next page. Maybe it isn't THORN at all, but MARMALADE or SPARROW. But for now it is THORN.

You should probably read on.

26

The last time I saw Ferdinand he was sitting on my porch, sleeping in one of my wicker chairs.

I was just out of bed, had barely had time to make myself a cup of coffee and throw on my satin morning robe. It was a beautiful day in an Indian summer that only seemed to last and last. Even so early, the sun was still blazing, all red and gorgeous. The wind that swept through my garden and caught the dry roses and apple tree leaves was sauna hot and felt like a caress, just the perfect day to take my morning coffee outside. I brought with me the manuscript that I never seemed to be able to finish editing and placed my glasses on top of my head. Armed thus with both pleasure and work, I stepped outside, and found him sleeping there, snoring softly with his mouth open, closed eyes aimed at the sky. His pale blue shirt was rumpled and large circles of perspiration had soaked through the fabric and spread out from his armpits. His red tie with little dogs on it was draped across his shoulder. His glasses were all askew.

I sat down on the other side of the table, put down my coffee carefully so I wouldn't wake him up. His car was haphazardly parked with one tire nearly grazing my magnolias. I wasn't in a hurry to know why he had come and promptly fallen asleep on my porch. I knew it couldn't be good. It probably had to do with Mara, and a part of me just didn't *want* to know. So I delayed the moment, took out my pink ink pen and started working on my book, circling words or crossing them out, penning small notes to myself on the pages. The coffee was good. The weather was fine. Ferdinand slept on.

When he finally woke up, with a backache no doubt, the sun was trailing toward the horizon, ready to set. He woke with a start, sat up in the chair, and fumbled with his glasses to set them straight. 'I'm sorry,' he mumbled, 'I'm sorry . . .'

'What are you so sorry for?' I had just had a lunch-slash-dinner; the empty plate stood before me on top of the manuscript sporting a piece of lettuce and a lemon slice.

'I don't know. For falling asleep? I didn't mean to, I swear . . .'

'No harm in that, but now that you're awake, some coffee?'

He brushed invisible lint off his clothes and nodded vigorously. I left him alone for a moment then, to go inside and pour him a cup. Pepper-Man was in the kitchen, leaning against the counter, waiting for me.

'What does he want?' He nodded in the direction of the porch.

'I don't know yet.' I poured the coffee. 'We'll have to see, won't we? Wait for him to talk.'

'Why would he come to you with this, why not your mother? You do not owe him your aid.' Pepper-Man seemed edgy – restless, worried perhaps.

'I am his sister and Mara is my daughter. He can see the faeries too, so where else would he turn?'

'I would not know, but he upsets you, and I do not like to see you upset.'

'Maybe you should talk to Mara about that. She is the one who causes the upset.'

'Mara ceased listening years ago, as you well know.'

'Exactly. The only way to prevent more damage is to hear my brother out, and help him if I can.'

'But I can feel the clouds gathering, Cassie. He smells like blood and fear, that man.'

'Not even you can know the future. Maybe this time we can quench the fire before it even begins.'

He shook his head. 'Hardly, it is already burning.'

'That is just *her* you feel.'

'Yes, it is, and that man out there, he will burn with her too.'

'That man still has nightmares about you, whatever harm could he do?'

'Tommy Tipp was a harmless man too, but think of all the grief and sorrow that he brought.'

'That was different.' I fetched Ferdinand's mug off the counter. 'Tommy Tipp was you.'

Out on the porch, I served my brother coffee and sat down before him.

'She came back,' he said, as I knew he would.

I stifled a sigh, suddenly feeling so old and weary. 'Go on.'

'She came back when I was playing, but this time I had locked the doors, so she knocked . . .'

'And?'

'I let her inside, I couldn't help it – she's my *niece*, and I think I am a little ashamed – no, *a lot* ashamed, that we have treated her so badly, even if none of us knew she was there.'

'Of course you feel that way, but you couldn't have known, and even if you invited her to Sunday dinner, she wouldn't really *be* there, you know.'

'But what *is* she, then? What *are* the faeries?' His eyes were wide open, pleading with me.

'They are nothing,' I told him. 'Nothing we can define.

205

They live in the cracks and narrow spaces, in between day and night. They are twilight people. Not quite dead, not quite alive.'

'Thank you,' he said solemnly. 'That was very helpful.'

I chuckled a little. 'You asked and I answered. You and I are pale fruit, brother, growing in the twilight. I always thought I was the only one of us who did, but it turns out you live there too. We're not quite at home in any world, and so we are meat for the faeries.'

'It doesn't seem to bother you, though.'

'It did – it does, but there's no use fighting it. A man born without an arm doesn't spend the rest of his life wishing for an arm, he learns to use the one arm that he has. That's what I do. I learn to be good with what I have – and maybe that one arm is enough, you know. Maybe you can do tricks with that arm; fantastic things no one has ever seen before. That's how you have to think about it, as a disability you can live with and maybe even transform into a strength.'

'Mara doesn't think so.'

'My daughter has never known any differently, and she doesn't know what she's wishing for.'

'She feels bereft.'

'That she does.'

'She says that if she could, she would be like me – us – and come live with me in my house.'

'You don't want that, Ferdinand, you really don't.'

'There must be a way, though, if she wants it so badly. You did it with Tommy Tipp, he was a faerie all along.'

'Then Mara would have to eat someone's heart first, like Pepper-Man did with Tommy's, and as you know, the spell didn't last, even though Pepper-Man is strong and old.'

'She seems so mad for being what she is, and mad for even

being born. Guilty, I think, for growing inside you when it clearly wasn't your choice.'

'She thinks I took her to the mound to hide her, but I took her there so she could live. She wasn't fit for this world, Ferdinand – I lost her.'

'In *Away with the Fairies: A Study in Trauma-Induced Psychosis*, Dr Martin says that it was they who did it, Mother and Father . . .'

'How did Mother feel about that, you reading the book?'

'She didn't feel a thing, she doesn't know.'

'Why *did* you read it?'

'To understand, I think. Not only the things that happened to you, but the things I remembered from childhood too. That *thing* . . .'

'Pepper-Man.'

'Yes, that *thing* . . .'

'That thing is probably listening in, I think you should know that. He wants me to not get involved this time, wants you and Mara to figure things out.'

'Why?'

I shrugged. 'He cares for me.'

'As well he ought to if you are the thing that lets him live.'

'It's not that easy, Ferdinand. He could easily have found himself another source of life, but these bonds run deep, my brother. You could almost confuse them with love.'

'You can't love *him*. He abused you as a child, took advantage of you always . . .'

'Well' – I squinted my eyes against the sun – 'they all do, don't they? Given a chance?'

'*They* who?'

'People, faeries – we all have to live. It's a predatory world out there. We all eat something, don't we? We hardly ask the piglet before we roast it and serve it with gravy.' This had become my favorite metaphor.

'I can't believe you'll compare yourself to a pig roast.'

'Well, there you have it. I'm very pragmatic.'

'But those stories about Mother and Father – especially *him* – are they true? Mara seems to think they are.'

'What do *you* think?' I shaded my eyes with my hand.

'I don't know what to think. In the book there are two stories, and now that I know for sure that Pepper-Man is real, I mostly want to believe that *he* did it – got you pregnant . . .'

'That would put Mara firmly in the mound.'

'Yes, it would, wouldn't it?' He seemed to think it over. 'There would be no point in thrashing against her confines, then, if Pepper-Man was her father for real.'

'She chose to believe Dr Martin, though, even if she didn't like him.'

'A faerie believing in a man, huh? Somehow that strikes me as odd.'

'Nevertheless, that's what she did.'

'And you, Cassie? Are you still confused?'

I took a moment. 'Maybe I have decided that it doesn't matter. Maybe one thing being true doesn't mean that the other thing is *untrue*.'

'How very faerie of you,' he replied. 'How very in-between.'

'That's how we do it, us twilight fruits. We decide not to decide, because as soon as you do, something happens that changes things again. It's better to stand firmly in the middle.'

'So you don't share Mara's thirst for revenge?'

'Whatever good would that do? It won't make her human.

It won't take her out of the mound.' It cut my heart to say it out loud.

'What do you think my niece will do?'

'You tell me, it's you she seeks out. You are the one she envisions as an accomplice.'

'Do you really think so?'

'I do.'

'Should I offer her to feed of me? Wouldn't that make her more human, make her more like me?'

'Why would you want to do that?'

'Well, it's not like I do much good in life, at least I'd be useful to *someone* that way.'

'And vulnerable, too. Look what happened to me.'

'But would it help her?' His eyes were imploring.

'Honestly? I think she's too angry for quick solutions. Even if she discarded her hawk for you, she would still have that seething fury, and it would only backfire on you, Ferdinand. It could cause you so much pain.'

'If I gave her my heart, though, so she could live in a body resembling mine for a little while?'

'You would give her your heart to eat?'

'Yes.'

'Why would you want that, Ferdinand? It's not your fault that she is like she is.'

'She came to me, didn't she? Reached out to ask for help.'

'Do you value your life so little?'

'. . . I might think that hers is worth more.'

I saw it all so clearly then, why Mara went to see him. She must have watched him, followed him around, and seen that he was ripe for just that kind of thing. He was a man without a purpose, a knight without a cause, a gentle soul with a big heart and a conscience heavy with guilt. She could use that, Mara. Could use a man willing to put his heart – literally – in her hands. He was like clay to her, moldable and soft. She could forge a warrior out of him, a servant loyal to the bone.

'Don't let her use you,' I said; my lips felt stiff and my mouth was dry. 'Don't let her talk you into anything.'

'I truly want to help—'

'It's not your fault what happened when we were children. Our father's brutality is not your sin, not our mother's viciousness either. You couldn't have saved me. You couldn't have spoken up. Even if you had insisted about Pepper-Man they wouldn't have believed you – or they'd just blame me for feeding you lies. There was nothing you could have done, brother, so please don't break your neck trying to make it right.'

He was quiet for a while. 'She is so horribly alone, though, even among her own kind.'

'Aren't we all?' My voice was dry.

'But Mara *needs* me,' he tried.

'As the spider needs the fly.'

'She is your daughter, Cassie. How can you speak of her like that?'

'I have known her all her life and loved her with all my heart, so I should know what she's like.'

'But if I want to help her—'

'Don't.'

'But if I want to—'

'Don't.'

He gave me a sad and accusing stare. 'Is that all you are going to say?'

'Yes. I know these beings better than you do and I know what a life is worth. Don't throw yours away on some useless agenda. My daughter is misguided, that is all. She should never have come to you.'

It was with a sickening feeling in my gut that I let him leave that evening. Pepper-Man came to hold me as we watched his taillights disappear down the road.

'So it has begun, then,' my lover said.

'I'd rather say that it has.' I startled when I heard the exhaustion and fear in my own voice.

'He is willing to commit, then, to Mara and her cause?'

'She has him so hard wrapped up around her little finger that I'm surprised he can still walk and talk without her aid. He has nothing, you know – nothing that he values above all.'

'Now he has her.'

'Yes, and I can only imagine what she tells him, that no one can help her but him, that he is the glimmer of hope in a world that ruined her and left her out in the woods . . .'

'She will break that man.'

'She will suck him dry.'

'Maybe, if he's lucky, he will die.'

We were quite proud of our girl, Pepper-Man and I.

***

I've often wondered what Dr Martin would have said if he'd been alive to witness what followed. How he would have tried to twist and bend the story to make it abide by his truth. Doubtless he would have called Mara my weapon, a piece of myself that I didn't want to be, so I separated myself from it, calling it my daughter.

My daughter who brought on my revenge.

Only she didn't, though, did she? It is not *her* name in the police reports, neither is it mine. It's only his – Ferdinand's. She used him so I wouldn't bleed.

I know that now.

Ferdinand couldn't say anything by then, not to defend himself, not to defend me, not to defend his niece – my brother was good and utterly dead.

I remember his casket: pale pine. Mother wasn't at the crematorium, she probably couldn't bear to be there. It was only me, the funeral director, and two men from the police. It seemed such a sad ending for a gentle soul. I hope he comes back, soaring like a dove, but I don't think that he will. He never struck me as the type to fight for life, to cling to it with all his might – rather he was the opposite of that, all too ready to let his life go, give it all up for my daughter's mad agenda.

***

Dr Martin would have said it was I, and not Mara, who talked my brother into it. That I used our shared history of abuse to manipulate him and force his hand. That is what Olivia thought, once she'd been forced to give up the idea that it was I alone who'd done the deed. She said I had spun poor Ferdinand in with my lies, and spat him out again, broken and cruel. For her, all evil comes from me. It never even occurred to her, I think, that Ferdinand might have had his own reasons, that I hadn't been the only one to suffer in that house. Your mother wouldn't know anything about that, though, tender little tangerine-marzipan girl that she is.

She'll never know the taste of pale fruit.

27

I know what you are thinking now: if I was so convinced that Mara would do something bad, why didn't I do more to stop her?

Well, I did – did all I could – everything within my might. That night, after Ferdinand left the lilac house for the last time, Pepper-Man and I walked out to the mound. We found Mara by the brook, cleaning her teeth with a crow's bone.

'I know why you are here,' she said upon seeing us. 'But there really is no need. I won't listen to your advice, no matter how wise you think it is.'

'Why?' I asked. 'Why is this so important to you? Why can't you just let those people be?'

'*Those people* are your family – and mine, too. If I don't deal with them, who will?'

'No one will, that's the whole point. No one will be dealing with anyone—'

'Why not?' She looked me square in the eyes.

I suddenly felt lost for words, I didn't quite know what to tell her. Maybe it was my upbringing, some deep-set fear and loathing, or a habit of keeping quiet that made me so reluctant to touch the subject of family, of *them*, and the deeds that went on in the white room.

'Ferdinand hasn't done anything. He is blameless, and still he's offering you his heart.'

'And I am very grateful for it too.'

'*Why* do you want him? What are you planning?'

'Are you worried that I'll bite?'

'I know what you are capable of, Mara, I don't need a demonstration. But why him? Why Ferdinand? The softest man alive . . .'

'Because he wants to.' She dropped the bone and stretched out her legs. 'He wants me to come and infuse his petty life with blood. He wants to *feel* something, Mother . . . anything will do.'

'And what will he do for you? What's the purpose of it all?'

'If I told you, you would try to stop me, and what is the fun in that?'

'There's no fun in any of this, that's what I'm trying to tell you. Revenge I can understand, Mara, but the destruction of an innocent—'

'No one is innocent,' she said lazily, fingers trailing the mossy ground. 'You have taught me that yourself.'

'He only wants to help you—'

'I know.'

'Stop this, Mara, before it's too late.'

'Too late for what, Mother? It's already too late.' She jumped up to her feet, eyes blazing. 'Here I am, cast aside like a rag doll to the mound. Never have I tasted salt, never have I shared your roof, never have I felt the sun upon my brow . . . I was gone before I even began! I was nothing from the start! You should have let me stay that way: nothing!'

I shook my head, utterly confused. 'How can you say that? At least there was life, and we loved you so much, ever since you came—'

She laughed then, dry and bitter like autumn leaves. 'You

could have spared yourselves the effort. What is born of cruelty begets cruelty. You cannot love darkness back to light, can't love death back to life. What is dead is dead, what is hate will hate. I was born to this, Mother. I was born to be your spear.'

'No!' It was as if she slapped me. My chest ached as my heart split open, flooding me with bitter salt. I gathered my cardigan close to my body and wiped tears from my eyes with the back of my hand. 'You were born to be mine,' I said in a whisper, 'you were born to be my daughter, and I will love you and cherish you and keep you close always.'

She stood before me, straight as a rod. 'I am your voice, when you will not speak.'

'I spoke in Dr Martin's book—'

'I am your hand when you won't make a fist.'

'It is so pointless, Mara. Anger gets you nowhere—'

'I am your knife, when you will not cut.'

'It will ruin you, Mara, I know it will – you should never go near that evil man.'

'But I will,' she said, 'when you won't.'

Pepper-Man had stood back until then; now he approached us by the brook. I remember the water dancing down the stream, the night air still heavy with heat. Above us hung the ripe full moon, a large pale fruit, like me.

'She said she didn't want you to,' Pepper-Man said to my daughter. 'She doesn't want you near that man – nor her brother, Ferdinand.'

'She has no right to tell me no. They are my kin too, I have a say in the matter.'

'No. How could you? They are boiling flesh and blood, you are dry as a root. You have no say. You have no life.'

Every word he said hit me like a fist. They were cruel words. Harsh words. Mara seemed to crumble before him. Then she hissed from deep within her chest:

'Say you, child thief. Say you, who led her by the hand into the woods, when she was nothing but a little girl. Say you, who guided her every step of the way, until you took her husband's place – stole life of your own, when you had none. Dare you tell me what I can and cannot do?' And then she went for his throat, I swear. She flung herself at him with teeth bared, hands like claws, slashing. Her skirts billowed, her legs barely touched the ground, her eyes shone with rage. He flung her aside with the back of his hand, a sound like the crack of a whip. She flew through the air, all across the brook, and landed in the thicket of junipers. There she crouched on the ground, staring at us across the water; eyes searing, searing with heat.

I ached for her then, I ached . . . that pain she felt, that *pain* . . .

'Well, have him, then,' I whispered, not really knowing if she'd hear me or not. Not really knowing which 'he' I meant. 'Have him, then, if it can help you . . . help you ease that pain.'

Pepper-Man held his hand pressed to his neck where her nails had grazed his skin. The dark matter underneath his hide peeked through the half-moon imprints she'd left.

I felt guilty too, I suppose, for bringing her into this world, to a life she didn't want. Born of pain – born in shame. Maybe she was right, maybe it was up to her to decide, end it the way she saw fit.

'Come' – I took Pepper-Man's hand in mine – 'leave our daughter to it.'

'But Ferdinand—'

'Is a grown man. Nothing we can do can help him now, not if he's decided to quit living the lie.'

And that is how it was, Janus and Penelope, there was nothing more we *could* do. Nothing but sit back and wait for the sirens, wait for the storm to hit. And when it did – when it did, *what* a storm it was.

What beautiful and blazing spears of lightning.

28

It was a tabloid reporter's dream, that's what it was, the abrupt end of our family. The violence struck out of nowhere – or that's what they thought, anyway. The two caskets so differently treated: surrounded by flowers and nothing at all. Two bodies in the ground.

Your mother might have told you about it, or you read it in the newspapers. You will know how our father was found down there in the bear pit, wooden spikes pinning him in place, and that huge red hole in his chest where the spear went in – came out. I suppose you imagined what it looked like, your grandfather splayed on spikes. I never saw it myself, but I too can imagine: red rims in his beard, red in his eyes, red on his gray-striped pajama shirt. The rifle by his side down there – useless. Where his heart ought to be, there was just gristle and flesh, torn and broken, red, pink, and white.

Spear went in – came out.

I told you before that the day on the porch was the last time I saw my brother, but it wasn't the last time I spoke to him. He called me the night of the murder, just after it was done. That's why I wasn't surprised at all when the police came knocking on my door. He called to warn me, I think, about it all.

'It's over,' Ferdinand said when I picked up the phone. His voice was bubbling with jubilant excitement.

'What is?' I felt cold.

'He is dead! I watched him go myself.'

'Oh no,' I breathed – not from sorrow, mind you, but from the implications of it all, what it would do to my girl – what it would do to him. A little piece of me even wondered what it would do to *me*. In my mind's eye, I saw it again: the hospital bed, the sad tray of food and the white, bitter pills in a plastic cup. 'What did you do?' I asked Ferdinand. 'What did *she* do?'

'She trapped him.' He sounded amazed.

'Trapped him, how?'

'She came to me last night. Wanted me to help her dig a hole in my garden.'

'A hole, huh?'

'Yes, and I did. It was fun.'

'Digging a hole isn't "fun", my brother. I think you may have had far too little fun in your life.'

'With her it was,' Ferdinand insisted. 'We laughed, and we sang, and she told me all these amazing stories—'

'I bet she did.'

'—about the woods and the mounds and the places she had gone with her hawk.'

'And?'

'Then I brought a bottle of wine outside, and I drank a few glasses while we whittled the spikes.'

'You drank wine while you crafted weapons to kill your father?' I didn't know if I should laugh or cry.

'Yes.' The exuberant tone in his voice had dwindled some. 'And we made holes for the spikes at the bottom of the pit, and planted the spikes down there.'

'Yes – and?'

'She cut down a young birch, removed all the bark, and made a spear out of it.'

'Really now?' I felt sick.

'Then dawn was coming and she said I was to get some sleep, because tonight it was all about to happen. She took the spear with her, I don't know what she did with it, but when she came back it was all black with letters—'

'From *Away with the Fairies: A Study in Trauma-Induced Psychosis*, no doubt.'

'Yes, how did you know that?'

'Oh,' I sighed. 'Just a hunch I had.' That book had become the very symbol of everything that she loathed. 'And then what happened, when she came back?'

'She told me to go and fetch Father. I was going to tell him there was an intruder on my – their – property. A *crazy woman*, she said. I was to tell him that there was a *crazy woman* . . .'

'And did you?'

'Yes. I let myself in with the spare key and woke him up, very careful so as not to wake *her* up. We didn't want Mother out there, it would only cause unnecessary trouble . . .'

'Of course.'

'He came at once, lumbering in his pajamas, even brought his old rifle along. He always liked a hunt, you know. When we came to the garden, though – he *saw* her, Cassie, I swear he did, dancing before him in the wane moonlight. She danced and she laughed and she egged him on. "Come and get me, old man – let's see if you still can, you vicious worm, you filthy bear . . ." She kept saying things like that. It was actually kind of vile, but I don't get how he saw her, Cassie . . .'

'The faeries have their ways . . .'

'Do you think he had the sight like us?'

'I doubt it.'

'But you don't know that for sure, do you?'

'No.'

'Anyway, he finally had enough of the teasing and came launching at her, bellowing from his chest. It was so loud and ugly I felt sure all the neighbors would wake up and come running.'

'But they didn't?'

'No, and not when he fell in, either, though the sounds he made then were even worse. Those screams, Cassie, those screams . . . and the mess down there . . . I didn't know there could be so much blood. Didn't know it could come from so many places at once. I think, Cassie' – his voice became brittle and shivering – 'I think it wasn't all real to me before then. I don't think I realized what I was part of – that we were actually going to do it . . . kill Father . . .'

'What did you think was going to happen? That you and Mara would sit out there under the moon drinking wine and whittling stakes just for the "fun" of it?' I couldn't keep my voice from shaking, couldn't keep the acid in check.

'No, I . . . I just didn't think—'

'No. You really didn't, did you?'

'But then she lifted the spear. It was already there, resting on the grass by the pit, and she took it in her hands and she ended the screaming. Easy like that, with one single blow. She must be terribly strong.'

'You're not saying . . .'

'I think she rammed it into his heart. There was a big, black hole there afterward, where his heart should have been – but wasn't.'

'Maybe he never had a heart?'

'I threw up then, in the flowerbed. My head was buzzing like crazy.'

'And she?'

'She laughed and declared them even. "A life for a life," she said, and then she took off, into the woods, as she does.'

'. . . As she does. And now you are stuck with a dead man in your garden. What are you going to do about that?'

'Fill in the pit, I think. Fill it in and plant some bulbs. It'll be a nice tulip patch in the spring.'

'Easy as that, huh?'

'What else am I to do? Call the police? Call Mother?'

'What does Mara say?'

'Nothing. She hasn't been back since she left for the woods.'

'She might be, though, brother, and if she does come back, please don't let her in.'

'Why not?' Again that shiver in his voice. Maybe on some level, he too knew that after the night they'd just shared, Mara wasn't safe company for him. 'You ought to be pleased, though,' he said at last, when the silence between us stretched, 'even if just a little . . .'

'Why?'

'The bear is gone, her pain has ended.'

'If you really think that, you're a fool. Pain like that doesn't go away, and *she* is the fool for thinking that it would. The rush from the kill will end, and what then? She still has a very long life to live.'

'I won't be sorry that I helped her, though.' He sounded like a child.

'Not yet,' I warned him. 'You're not sorry *yet*. Doesn't mean you won't be.'

'Doesn't mean I will.'

'As you wish.' I gave up. 'I'm sure you feel like quite the knight, but hurry up, now, your night isn't over. You still have a hole to fill in.'

'Yes, yes, it really wouldn't do if Mother came over and saw him down there.' Again, there was that shiver.

'No, my dear brother, it certainly wouldn't.'

'I didn't expect there to be so much blood, and those sounds that he made—'

'Go, go, go – fill in that hole!'

'Yes, Cassie, you're right, I should go. I should go fill it in. I'll do that now.'

'Good, Ferdinand, you do that now.'

And that was the last time we spoke.

***

He never did fill in that hole, though, did he? Something happened between the time we hung up and the time he was found that prevented him from going outside to finish the job.

Could it have worked?

Maybe.

Maybe filling it in and planting tulips was just the right choice.

Maybe Mother would have thought that Father had left her, ignoring the fact that his valet and jacket were still there, the car in the garage, and—

No, it wouldn't have worked.

From the moment he chose to wear Mara's colors, Ferdinand was lost. There was no coming back from what he did – no coming back from what he'd witnessed. It's hard, being the knight of a harsh queen.

As it was, however, it didn't take Mother long to find her husband in her son's garden. According to the police and the newspapers, Mother woke up, found him gone, brewed some coffee, and threw on a shawl over her morning robe. Then she grabbed two cups and walked over to Ferdinand's to ask him if he had seen his father. At that time, I think, she still thought Father was out hunting pigeons, having seen the rifle missing from its rack. She took the shortcut through the gardens, not being properly dressed and all, planning to slip inside through the back door and wake her son with some fresh morning brew ... On her way there, her sharp eyes caught sight of something unusual: a pile of dirt that shouldn't be there; a freshly dug hole on the lawn. Wondering what that nonsense was about – the garden, she thought, was perfectly fine – she wandered over, balancing the cups, and looked down at that grisly scenario. Her husband was very much found, punctured and maimed by wooden spikes, and if he'd ever had a heart, it certainly wasn't there anymore.

Mother screamed, dropped the coffee, and ran to Ferdinand's patio doors, drumming with her fists on the glass, calling to Ferdinand to let her in. She had 'just found your father dead in the garden!' She didn't call it murder yet, mind you, didn't suspect even that her son was involved, though her husband was dead on his lawn. She *did* realize that he was dead, so there was never any question of medics or an ambulance. I guess that was due to the hole in his chest. You can't get much deader than that.

When Ferdinand failed to respond, she didn't go in through the back door as she had planned, she went back to her own house and called the police. I don't know what she said to them, only that it was logged as an accident at first. Mr Thorn had had an accident. When they arrived at the scene, though, it was quickly changed to murder. Not only was the bear pit a lethal trap in itself, but the weapon that had speared his heart was missing from the scene.

They knocked on Ferdinand's door several times during this first round of investigations, where the body was removed and the scene secured. He quickly became a person of great interest, and though Mother was both shaking and sobbing at the time, she readily agreed to let them inside, using Ferdinand's spare key.

They found him then, of course.

I have asked Mara many times what really happened that night; why he never filled that pit back up. She says she doesn't know, says she never went back – but I know that she is lying. I know that not only because the bloody spear was found beneath his hanging body, but because of the ring of mushrooms that had suddenly sprouted forth on his living room floor. They never told you about that, did they? About that sudden infestation of fungi in his house, those pearly white mushrooms that appeared overnight. Not there the day before, said the help. I only know because I went to Ferdinand's sad funeral, and overheard the police officers talking to each other. It didn't make sense to them – but it certainly did to me.

After they found Ferdinand, it was a clear-cut case to the police. Especially since the spear was inscribed with nasty quotes from Dr Martin's book. Ferdinand had taken it to heart, they said, that book had 'ruined his life' and become his truth, and so he killed our father with it.

Then he killed himself.

29

When the police finally arrived at the lilac house, noon had long since come and gone. I was sitting on my porch doing crossword puzzles, but really just watching the road. The day was chilly and I was wrapped in a knitted blanket, a cloud of steam rose from the tea before me. I'd felt sick to the core all day, felt it in my bones that something was doomed to turn out bad. I didn't know yet that he'd never filled in that hole with dirt. Neither did I know about Ferdinand's fate. As far as I was concerned, they might only think my father missing.

I soon learned it was more serious than that.

The police officer who was driving the vehicle was a big, red-bearded man that I remembered from my trial. He had been the first one on the scene after they discovered what they thought was Tommy Tipp. He'd been just a rookie then, slimmer and fitter, hair more lustrous and thick. His name was Officer Parks. The other police officer was a woman, fairly young and dark-skinned; she said her name was Amira. I think she was the one who was supposed to comfort me if I broke into pieces at the news.

They stood before the porch where I sat; Parks fiddled with his belt as cops do.

'Are you Cassandra Tipp?' asked Amira.

'She is,' Parks grunted beside her.

'I'm afraid we have some bad news for you,' said Amira. 'Can we come inside or – come sit down there with you?'

I nodded, didn't like where this was going. 'What is it?' My voice was high-pitched as I battled jolts of fear. 'What has happened?'

The two officers took their time approaching me, then sinking down in my wicker chairs.

'Mrs Tipp,' Amira said. 'I am sorry to inform you that your father and your brother passed away last night.'

'What?' I burst out – hadn't seen that coming. Not the part about Ferdinand, anyway. 'Why? What happened?'

'We are not sure yet.' Amira looked weary. 'Your father was found in your brother's garden, and his death was . . . quite violent. Unfortunately, everything points to your brother being involved in his death, including his subsequent suicide.'

'Suicide, huh?' I murmured, thinking thoughts better left unspoken.

'You mother doesn't think so.' Parks's dark eyes stared unblinkingly across the table. He remembered me well, then. Remembered Tommy Tipp. 'She thinks you may have had a hand in this.' He ignored Amira's warning gaze. 'That you're somehow responsible for them both.'

'Me? Why? I barely spoke to any of them for the last thirty years or so.'

'So you weren't aware of any disagreement between them?' Amira's cheeks were flushed, from shame on Parks's behalf, I reckoned.

'No, I'm not on speaking terms with any of them. You can ask anyone – I'm surprised Mother even remembers my name.'

'Your mother is quite determined' – Parks again – 'that your brother would have had help. Your father died violently, as we said, and certain skills were involved that your mother is very certain that your brother didn't possess. Like woodcarving and weaponry.'

'He did fence for a while,' I tried to be helpful. 'But as I said, I didn't know him well, so I don't know who could have helped him.'

'You write books about a lot of different things, though, don't you? You have to *know* a lot of things to do that,' Parks plowed on. Amira's cheeks stayed flushed.

'I certainly write very little about woodcarving and weaponry. I write mostly about beaches and fruity drinks.'

'You are no stranger to human anatomy, though.'

'Well, my stories sometimes get heated, but as you well know, Officer Parks, I have been a widow for quite some time.'

'You know very well what I mean.' The beard bobbed on his chest while he spoke.

'Tell me how my brother died.' I was eager to get them back on track.

'He hanged himself from the roof beam,' grunted Parks.

Amira mumbled, 'So sorry . . . so sorry . . .'

'The murder weapon was found in there with him,' said Parks. 'It has scribbles all over it, quotes from that book about fairies.'

'Huh?'

'That book about fairies, the one he wrote, the doctor who treated you.'

'Dr Martin?'

'That's the one, and your mother swears the scribbles on the spear are in *your* hand.'

'It is messy, though,' added Amira, 'hard to tell with all the . . . matter.'

'I'm sure my mother has quite forgotten what my loops and curlicues look like by now.'

'We are so sorry to bring such bad news,' Amira burst out, 'and so sorry we have to ask all these questions.'

'As I said, we weren't close.'

'Still . . .'

'Ours wasn't a happy home.' I was still trying to throw them off the scent – using the truth, no less. 'When we grew up there was much discord. You can read all about it in "the book about fairies".'

'Thank you,' said Amira, 'we'll do that.'

Parks only grunted in reply.

***

'Why the heart?' I asked Mara when she finally reappeared, sitting in my kitchen as if nothing had happened, flipping through a wildlife magazine.

'It is a very effective way of killing.'

'Seems like a lot of work, though, digging that pit, whittling those stakes . . .'

'He was a big man and I didn't want to take any chances. Down there he was pretty much stuck – you don't walk away from a position like that. It works perfectly fine with real bears as well.'

'And what about Ferdinand?'

'What about him?'

'Well, he died, didn't he?'

'It appears so.'

'He killed himself, Mara, and that isn't good.'

'He should have filled in the pit first.'

'Yes, he should have – why didn't he?' I slumped down in the chair opposite her, gently took the magazine from her hands so she was forced to look at me. On the glossy pages, stags were fighting, locking antlers in a tangle of bones.

'I don't know,' she shrugged. 'He got frightened maybe. I think seeing it made him feel bad.'

'Well, yes, it would, wouldn't it? A grown man spiked and speared—'

'I never forced him to do anything.'

'But you went back there, didn't you? You were there when Ferdinand died.'

'I was not.'

'But the spear, Mara, and the mushrooms?'

'I left the spear behind when I left. As for the fairy ring, you should ask your lover.'

'Pepper-Man?'

'The very one.'

'Why would I want to do that?'

'Well, if I didn't do it, who else has such high stakes in this they went to your brother and strung him up . . . left footprints on the floor . . .'

'Oh no,' I said. 'You can't make me blame Pepper-Man for this. You are only mad that he hit you.'

'Well, think about it, Mother. It was the best way to protect you, wasn't it, to firmly plant the guilt with him – with Ferdinand . . . And who is more eager to protect you in the whole wide world than the very creature that feeds from you?'

'You are cunning, my daughter, but I won't play along. Not this time. Pepper-Man knew I didn't want Ferdinand harmed—'

'When did he ever care about what you want? He is self-serving in every way, you have said so yourself, many times. If

Pepper-Man thought it was better if he died, your *feelings* really didn't matter.'

'He wouldn't do that to me—'

'Yes, he would.'

'He is your father—'

'No, he's not. I don't have a father. Not anymore.' A tiny smile played on her lips. I looked at her for a while then, the unruly hair, the tattered feathers. My daughter – dark sister – born of pain.

'You should have filled in that hole,' I said weakly.

'What difference does it make now? Ferdinand is good and dead.'

'Do you remember the color of his tie when he died?'

'Blue, I think – with little birds on it.' She always had exceptional sight.

'Doves?' I asked, heart fluttering.

'Swallows, I think.' So much for poetry, for symbols and signs.

'What was the last thing he said to you?'

'He wasn't speaking, he was retching.'

'He wouldn't have brought that spear back inside.'

'No, he wouldn't, but Pepper-Man would, if he was to place the blame.'

I sat back, clasped my hands in my lap. I felt thoroughly and utterly defeated. 'Are you feeling better now, Mara? Do you feel like your revenge has made a difference in your life? Did it set you free as you hoped?'

She shrugged again. 'I never expected it to make much difference. It was just something that needed to be done.'

'Your "purpose in life", isn't that what you called it? So what now, when the deed is done?'

'Now' – she leaned back in the chair, stretched out her legs – 'I keep going.'

***

I remember discussing Mara with Dr Martin once. It was just after he released the book – was just a conversation, not a session.

'Do you think it was a coincidence that Mara was born after your trip to the clinic?' he asked me.

'Not at all. She was born then because else she would die.'

'Daughter, huh? *Shadow self* – does that term mean anything to you?'

'No.'

'It's like an evil twin that lives inside your mind; someone you don't want to relate to. It's a part of you, even if you don't want it to be. Sometimes it's small, barely there at all, other times it's strong and overpowering. It's where we put all our unwanted feelings and emotions; those destructive impulses we don't want to act on.'

'She does that, though. She acts on her impulses all the time.'

'Because you can't.'

'Because it's how she is.'

I wonder what he would have made of all this, Dr Martin. What questions he would have asked me had he known about the bear pit, the spear with his words on it, and the spinning body of a dove. I still pretend to hear him sometimes, hear him in my head:

'Isn't it possible, Cassie, that you talked to your brother about what happened in your shared childhood home, and that the two of you together came up with this plan, just like your mother and sister think?'

'No,' I would have replied. 'I never was one for vengeance.'

'Yet vengeance is the legacy you passed on to Mara, isn't it?'

'That was just bad luck,' I would say. 'I never wanted Mara to have to deal with it at all.'

'But didn't you, somewhere deep inside? Isn't it a very human quality to seek vengeance – or *justice*, as we call it these days? Isn't it fair to say that the need for restoration of ego and soul after a betrayal is so deeply embedded in us that the need will push forth, no matter how deep we bury it?'

'It depends on the person, I guess,' I would say then.

'Exactly . . . And you, Cassie, what kind of person are you? Are you the kind who can obliterate the need to strike back if you're hit, or will you just find other ways to do it?'

'Like having a vengeful daughter?'

'Just that. A daughter with a "warrior soul".'

'I never wanted this,' I would say again.

'No,' he would say then. 'But *she* did.'

30

I suppose you think me mild for not coming down on your cousin harder, but when you're dealing with faeries there is one thing you must understand: life goes on forever, and they are all stuck in the mound. They don't bear grudges for what happened last year, nor a hundred years ago. To me, that has always been one of the most appealing things about them, the way time flows and erases all that was – the only thing that matters is the here and now.

I used to find solace in that, it was my touching stone for years. My past didn't define me when I lived among the faeries; nothing that happened to me tainted me forever. Mara wasn't like that, though – was always looking back. I was hoping that the bear hunt would release her from all that; that she would be free now, and stop moving against the tide. It never even entered my mind to let our disagreement continue. What good would that do, arguing with my daughter? It wouldn't solve a thing, now that it was done. Ferdinand and Father were dead, and our continued disagreement wouldn't change that. The police would never be looking for clues among the roots and the stones, deep within the mound.

'She blames you,' I told Pepper-Man when Mara had left. 'She said it was you who strung up my brother and planted that spear by his feet.'

'Of course she would say that. She is angry because I hit her.'

'Did you, though? Did you kill my brother?'

He didn't answer me outright. 'I will always protect you and Mara, even when you do not want me to.'

'He was going to fill in that hole.'

'And plant tulips – yes, I know. But buried bones always whisper, Cassandra. Before he knew it, he would have had scores of flowers bleeding in his lap, their petals shaped like bears and hearts. It would spread like a toxin through the earth, taint everything it touched with rage and violence. Better he is buried properly. Better it is not a secret.'

'But Ferdinand—'

'Is at peace now, and that was what you wished for, was it not?'

I couldn't really argue with that. 'They still blame me, though, Mother and Olivia.'

'Of course they do. They would not be who they are if they did not.'

'She is *my* daughter, though, so I guess they have a point. If I hadn't taken Mara to the mound, none of this would have happened.'

'But, Cassandra, what difference does it make? Is the world a poorer place for your father not being in it?'

'But Ferdinand—'

'Was not fit for life.'

'He might have been, though, if—'

'It is done,' Pepper-Man spoke into my ear. 'It is over now, my Cassandra. It is done.'

And it was.

***

Father's funeral was a beautiful disaster, as disasters go. I didn't expect it to be any different, still I felt I had to go, to see him buried if nothing else.

The church was filled with flowers – white: roses, carnations, lilies. The casket was closed, as it ought to be, he wasn't a pretty sight, even when alive. His coffin was shiny and black amid the dull white, rested on a sheet of tulle. Mother's eyes were hidden behind a veil, it drooped from her pillbox hat like a black wave. Her hair was tied back with a black velvet bow; less curly now, less yellow, more a faded gray. Her suit was very chic, though; she still had a very slim figure. She sat between you, Penelope, and your mother. The latter was sporting a black dress and satin gloves, wore thin, high heels that made her seem tall. I remember you because you didn't wear black, but navy blue. Maybe your mother hadn't thought to buy you funeral clothes. The pearls you wore were old, and so was the ivory ring on your finger. I remember both well from my mother's box of gems. Passed on to you, then, I guess you have them still. She wanted to make sure, I think, that none of her finery ever came to me. Janus, I don't remember you at all. Maybe you were sick that day – or maybe I just didn't care to look.

I didn't sit down beside you in the front row. I squeezed in at the back, among his more distant acquaintances and neighbors from my childhood. My purple clothes and moonstone bangles made me stand out like an exotic orchid in the sea of black and somber charcoal. Those who knew me gave me strange looks. Wondering, I suppose, just why it was that I stood there in the back – yes, *stood*, because the church was crammed with people, quite possibly due to the dramatic circumstances – the *family tragedy*, as the newspapers called it. He really didn't have that many friends, but everyone wanted to come and look, at Mother, at you – the grieving family. *Survivors* is what you were, every last one of you. Survivors of a *family tragedy* that ended in blood and violence on Ferdinand's well-kept lawn.

Just as they came to look when Tommy Tipp died that second time.

It's just human nature. They really can't help themselves.

I remember the service as hot and smelling of perspiration caught in synthetic fabrics, generously mixed with the scent of roses and candle wax. About halfway through, my mother must have gotten the whiff of me somehow, because she kept turning back, looking. Her lips were thin and white behind the veil.

I kept my eyes on the casket, though; that was why I was there, to see him lowered in the ground, to see him disappear. See the result of my daughter's anger and assure myself it was true.

I wondered what his last thoughts were. Wondered if he ever realized who she was, that strange and beautiful girl who went out of her way to provoke him out there on the lawn. If he ever saw my face in her face, the family resemblance. And then, when he fell, and the world turned to pain – what did he think of then? Did he have time to think at all? Did he realize his life had come to an end, and did he understand why? Did he understand that his son had betrayed him?

We will never know the answers to those questions, of course, but I do like to think that he knew; that he understood, in those final few minutes of his life, that his time was up and the past came back for him – came for his heart with a spear full of words.

'Truth,' according to Mara.

'Lies,' according to some.

Outside the church, we all stood in a circle, watching the

casket go down in the ground. Words were said, dirt was thrown. *This* hole would be filled to the brim. Just beside the open grave, there was a naked patch of dirt in the grass. That's where Ferdinand's ashes were. They would rest side by side, then, united in death. Neither of them would have been thrilled to know that.

When it was all over and time to go home, Mother lifted her veil. Her eyes looked straight at me, blue as the autumn sky. I made to turn and walk away, but she called after me: 'Wait!'

I paused, watched as she battled herself free from well-meaning uncles and your mother, who tried to hold her back from me. She strode right toward me through the green grass, her blue gaze like cut glass.

'What did you do, Cassie?'

I smiled, not to be mean, but because I didn't know what else to do.

'It is lovely to see you, Mother—'

'Oh, don't you "Mother" me. I know what you are – I know you're insane, but not even I expected *this* . . .'

'Well, Mother, as you well know, it was Ferdinand and not I who—'

'Bullshit and you know it.' My mother was no longer watching her language. 'You made him believe in it, didn't you? Made him believe in that mad doctor's lies?'

'I never made anyone do anything.' People were moving all around us, mourners walking to their cars. I am sure they stared as they passed us by, sure they walked close to hear what we were saying, but I didn't pay attention to any of them. Her eyes like glass before me, it was impossible to look away.

'Of course you have,' said Mother. 'I know my children well. You are persuasive and he was weak – but I also know it wasn't your fault, Cassie. It was him all along, filling your head with those dreadful stories, molding everything to fit his dirty little mind.'

'Who? Father?'

'No! Dr Martin! Writing it all in that awful book. And now he has killed *my son*.' Suddenly her face cracked open, splintered and fell apart like a china doll ruthlessly smashed to the floor. Her mascara ran in black rivulets, leaving fat trails on her white-powdered skin. 'And now he has killed my *husband*,' she choked. 'And ruined *you*, Cassie, he ruined you, too. That awful man, he ruined you, too . . .' Her hand clutched at the air, trying to reach me, and I stepped back; I didn't want those coral nails on me; the wrinkled old fingers; the scent of gardenias . . .

I could see the uncles coming up behind her. Olivia stayed put, clutching her purse, looking at us with wide doe eyes. When the first uncle arrived and gently took Mother by the shoulders, I used the opportunity to take another step back, away from her and the confusing affection I suddenly saw in her eyes.

'It wasn't your fault,' she breathed, as they pulled her with them, away from me.

As reconciliations go, I guess it could have been worse, but it was not what I expected.

Not at all.

***

Do you remember any of this? That scene at the end of the funeral? What did Mother do after you left the grave? Did she cry, or freshen up in the car to see the day through, head held high?

Did she speak of me again – ever?

I walked by the old house a few years later and saw that there was another family living there. There were swings in the garden, a cat on the porch. Ferdinand's house too had new inhabitants, someone with a strong stomach, I presume, to live where it all went down.

I don't know where Mother went after she moved, but I reckon that you do. If she is still alive she must be well over ninety and tucked away in some home, I guess. Somewhere close to Olivia and maybe even you.

'It is not important,' Pepper-Man says when I bring it up, 'you will always have me.' And he is right about that, and wrong too.

***

'Maybe I didn't go to the clinic,' I say, when I fall into one of my retrospective moods. 'Maybe I only made that up. Maybe Dr Martin *helped me* make that up . . .'

'Why do you think of that? Why is it significant?' Pepper-Man asks.

'It is significant to *them*: to Mother, to Mara, and to Ferdinand too, who died . . .'

'Nothing is significant to the dead. They are gone.'

'You are not.'

'I am not like most dead.'

He will take my weary old feet in his hands then. His fingers are gnarled again, from age, not from sap. He massages the pads of my toes, the hard skin on my heels. He has changed some since Father died, become softer and kinder, gentler with me. Less of a faerie and more of a man, vulnerable and brittle with age. 'What is done is done,' he says, 'and it can never be undone.'

If the night is fair and I'm up for it, we take a stroll around the garden, pondering what was and what will be. Pepper-Man picks plums and apples from the branches and offers them to me; jewels of fall, sweet and taut with juice.

'What will happen later?' I ask, as we walk below the canopy of gnarled branches and glossy leaves, the rich taste of apples in my mouth. His hand is on my back, steadying my steps.

'You are growing weary now?'

'I am.'

'I will take you to the mound, then.'

'And . . . ?'

'You go inside.' He pauses and turns toward me, catches a wisp of my white hair between his fingers, rubs it as if to feel the texture, how it has withered since my youth.

'And then I don't come out again?' The sky above bleeds a twilight violet.

'No, not for a while. And when you do, you will be different.'

'Will I be like you then, taking life from the living?'

'What is life, Cassandra, really? Would you say I do not live?' He lifts the coil of hair to his lips and kisses it.

'You know what I mean.'

'Yes, you will be like me.'

'I will feed off a horse, then.' I imagine the wind through my hair as I race across a meadow.

'Your face would be horribly long. If you still care about such things, after.'

'A cat, then.' I imagine lustrous fur and whiskers.

'A cat would suit you fine.'

'Will you still be with me?'

Pepper-Man's gaze meets mine. His face is still smooth but ashen and worn; paler somehow, skin paper thin. His hair is dry and steely gray. 'We can both feed from cats, together.'

He might not have loved me at first, when he entered my world when I was a child, but he does now, I'll tell you that. It was nothing he expected, I'll tell you that too. I was simply a meal at first, a strawberry tart to chew on – but the heart, even a dead one, doesn't ask before it swells. He needs me, yes, but he loves me too.

Loves me even more than I do.

'I have known you for so long.' I reach up and let my fingers trail the outline of his face. 'It's like you are a part of me, of every breath I take.'

'Two peas in a pod,' he answers and laces his fingers with mine. 'I will always be with you, every step of the way, until your last breath is gone, and beyond.'

31

And now you have reached the end of me. The end of this body of words.

Janus, I bet you're groaning deeply, as you rise from the chair and stretch your stiff limbs. Penelope, you're just sighing, and let the last pages flutter to the floor. Nothing for you to do now, is there, but lock up the house and drive away, arrive at the solicitor's early tomorrow morning, fresh and ready after a good night's sleep, and there you will say the magic word: THORN, and the manila envelope is opened and the treasure is yours. Yes. All of it. You are my heirs, as I have no one else. You are my heirs – isn't that strange?

'But where *is* she?' Penelope may be asking, while looking at the pages on the floor. As if the innocent pink paper sheets can tell her.

Janus shrugs before he answers: 'I don't know.'

'Dead somewhere?' Penelope's gaze is drawn to the window, to the branches of the apple tree lashing at the glass, at the rivulets of moisture from the rain. Imagining my bones, perhaps, licked clean by wind and frost, covered in fungus and crawling with ants.

'She would have us believe she's off with the fairies,' Janus says. 'She would like us to believe that she has mounted the silver stag and entered the woods for the very last time, her fairy protector behind her, gray hair whipping in the breeze . . .'

'What do *you* think?' Penelope looks like a child in that moment, lips parted, eyes wide.

'I think the same as you, she was a very confused woman, and she died.'

'That is certainly what Mom would say.'

'And right she would be, too. Did you *read* the things she wrote?'

'But still.' Penelope is a little enchanted. A part of her always wanted to believe in faeries and ghosts. 'What if she is right and we are wrong?'

'Penelope, the woman was a *killer*.' While Janus speaks, his eyes scan the room. You flipped the light switch sometimes during your reading session, and a golden light spills from the brass chandelier in the ceiling, but the shadows still bleed from the corners. Shadows to hide in, to watch from. Faeries like the shadows best.

'I don't like this house very much.' A shiver runs down Penelope's spine. 'I just wish that we knew where she was.'

'I can't argue with that, it would certainly be comforting to have her safely buried.' In his mind, he sees me – well, not me, because he hasn't really seen me for a while, and doesn't know exactly what I look like, but some blue-haired woman in a faded pink cardigan running wild in his house with an axe.

'She went through so much, there's so much pain in there.' The tip of Penelope's high-heeled shoe gently touches the pages on the floor. 'At least I hope her death was painless – *if* she is dead, that is.'

'Of course she is.' Janus would rather think of me that way, and erase the axe murderer from his mind.

'Why didn't they find her, then?' Penelope is thinking of the search party that doubtlessly combed through the woods last autumn. 'Why are there no traces of her body?'

'Because she went into the fairy mound?' Janus is aiming for sarcasm, but the tremble in his voice gives him away. He is frightened of the mound. The idea of a place like that gives him the shivers, touches something tender in him that makes him feel things he hasn't felt for years: that the night is vast and very dark and something lives in the closet.

Penelope speaks. 'Uncle Ferdinand, though . . . do you think—'

'I don't know, Penny . . . *Something* certainly happened there, but we will never know the truth.'

'Mom blames *her*, Aunt Cassie is right about that.'

'Mom *always* blames her. I don't think she is very rational either, when it comes to this whole dratted mess. If a fuse pops or she runs out of hot water, what does she do? She curses Aunt Cassie, as if her sister was some evil witch, cooped up in the woods muttering spells. That whole generation of our family is deranged, if you ask me . . . At least Aunt Cassie made some money from it.'

'Thorn.' Penelope says the password out loud, as if to test it on her tongue.

'Just that. Let's just hope she hasn't fooled us . . . Even if she *is* alive, running about the woods somewhere, we have done everything by the book. We have legal claim to that money, all her instructions are followed to the letter.'

'I know.' Penelope's gaze has glazed over, looks out in the room, dreamy and soft. It makes her brother worried.

'You don't really believe it, do you? That she had a super-natural companion and visited the *fairies*? Come on, Penny, don't buy into the madness.'

'It would explain a lot.' The poor girl is halfway down the rabbit hole already.

'No, it wouldn't. It wouldn't even make sense! Why would there be a fairy mound in the woods surrounding S—? With thousand-year-old, *dead* people in it, no less. Where did they come from? Were there even people here a thousand years ago?'

'Maybe they can travel.' Her eyes are shiny with excitement, spots of red have appeared on her cheeks. 'Maybe the fairies can move and resettle like everyone else.'

Janus shakes his head. 'Careful now, Penny. You really don't want to end up like Aunt Cassie—'

'I'm only saying that it would be neat if it *did* exist.'

'Would absolve Aunt Cassie from all the crimes, wouldn't it?'

'Would absolve us all, I reckon . . . I'm not saying that Dr Martin was right about everything, but Uncle Ferdinand snap-ping like that . . . Maybe there *was* something to what the old man wrote?'

'Never let Mom hear you speak like that.'

'Mom is old and biased. Maybe we should be open to new perspectives.'

'Like the ones Aunt Cassie proposes? Fairy magic and angry dead daughters?'

'Maybe, maybe not . . . but we may at least be open to the possibility that something was rotten in Grandmother and Grandfather's house.'

'It always looked normal to me, if a little stiff.'

'Yes, they weren't the kindest of people.'

'Didn't make them child molesters, though.'

'It just seems a little too easy to blame it all on Aunt Cassie. How much damage can one person wreak, even a slightly insane one?'

'Quite a lot. Look at Hitler.' Janus thinks himself very clever.

'It had to have come from somewhere, though. All those ideas she had – they had to come from *somewhere*.'

'Or not. The mind is a curious thing, and she has a shelf full of books to prove that she was capable of making things up.'

'Let's pretend for a moment that she was right – that she really paired up with Pepper-Man and that everything she wrote is true. Where would Aunt Cassie be now?' Penelope just can't let go.

'Hibernating in the mound, I guess, waiting to be reborn as a fairy.'

'And Mara? Do you think she's still around? Do you think she visits this house?'

'No. She isn't real so she isn't here, or anywhere else for that matter.'

'It's a cruel and horrible story.' Penelope shudders. 'It must have been terrible living with a truth like that, even if it wasn't true.'

Janus collects the sheets of paper littering the desk. 'Be that as it may, it's not really up to us to judge, we have done what she asked and now it's time to collect.'

'You really think that's enough? To step into the solicitor's office and say the word?'

'That is what it says.' His knuckles hit the stack of paper.

Penelope looks a little confused. 'It seems so easy. After all this – just too easy.'

And right she is.

I am pleased that you have read this far, even if you have discovered the password. You could have been on your merry way right now, manuscript in the trash, password dancing at the tip of your tongues, ready to be spit out and used. There *is* a catch, of course there is – it *would* be too easy if there weren't. I can see what you are thinking now, but don't you worry, hatchlings, I won't have you swearing off your mother or make you clear my name or any such nonsense. The catch has to do with the money itself.

It is faerie money.

Every last penny in my account is earned from the gifts they gave me, and as I told you before, it comes with a price. Every gift of Faerie does, even by extension.

The money is, quite literally, cursed.

If you choose to believe I am mad as a dog, and that every word I say is the raving of a lunatic – then by all means, be my guest. Take the money and be on your way.

If you believe I told you the truth, though – even if just a part of you does – you better think twice about this gift. It certainly comes with baggage.

The money won't turn to leaves and stones like in the faerie stories of old. It isn't that kind of faerie coin. Instead, it comes with faeries – how is that for passing on my legacy?

Everyone who keeps or spends from my funds will draw faeries to their home like a magnet. It's an invitation, that money of yours, a path of breadcrumbs straight to your doors.

Penelope, when you come home tomorrow, after a taxing day at the bank depositing all that money, a red-eyed man with wings like a bat will sit perched outside your window looking in. He'll see you, your red lips, your high heels, and he'll want to own every part of you, wrap you up tight in his leather embrace, taste your dark blood and swallow your soul.

Janus, when you enter the shower after kissing your children goodnight, a water girl will be in there with you, ready to soap up your back. She'll whisper stories in a tinkling voice like sunlight dancing on a brook, tell you what you taste like: blood and bone and marrow. She'll cradle your daughters and sing them to sleep, tell them about how nice it is, dwelling in that cold, dark stream, and there won't be anything you can do to stop her.

And that, my friends, is just the beginning. Soon there will be wizened leaves in your coffee, twigs in your pancakes, and mushrooms in your beds. The money comes with faeries, or it doesn't come at all.

It is your choice, really. Your choice to make.

Believe and be safe. Don't and be damned.

Maybe.

Acknowledgements

When I had just finished the first draft of *You Let Me In*, I read it over, and immediately decided that it was too strange to ever get published. Thankfully, I let someone else read it before I put it away. If it hadn't been for the wonderful Liv Lingborn, who told me, in her sternest voice, that this was The One, and to get on with it, this novel would have led a sad and lonely existence on my hard drive, never to see the light of day. Needless to say, I'm very grateful, not only for the rescue, but also for her valuable feedback on the first drafts. I couldn't have asked for a better friend to hold my hand through this process.

I'm deeply grateful to my amazing agent, Brianne Johnson, for believing in me and my strange little novel; for her editorial help and guidance, and for deftly introducing me to the nuts and bolts of publishing. I'm also grateful to Peggy Boulos Smith, Alexandra Levick, and everyone else at Writers House who has worked on *You Let Me In*'s behalf.

A heartfelt thank you goes out to my editor Miriam Weinberg, who saw the potential and helped me make this novel the best that it could be, and to everybody else at Tor who has helped make this book a reality. Likewise, a big thank you to my UK editor, Simon Taylor, and the rest of the team at Transworld. You have all made this awkward Norwegian's landing a smooth one.

ACKNOWLEDGEMENTS

I also owe thanks to my cats, whose habit of bringing in debris inspired this novel in the first place, and to my son, Jonah, whose patience and support is endless. Know that I am grateful.

Lore dictates that one should never thank the faeries, so I'll refrain from doing that – just in case . . .

About the Author

Camilla Bruce was born in central Norway and grew up in an old forest, next to an Iron Age burial mound. She has a master's degree in comparative literature and has co-run a small press that published dark fairy tales. Camilla currently lives in Trondheim with her son and cat. *You Let Me In* is her first novel.